## Nick Carter at Work

Behind the pole, Dok craned his neck to see what Carter had thrown out, but could not.... He saw the dead driver, and then Carter's head, where he was crouched on the other side of the car....

Carter raised the Luger in an unhurried way, aimed it carefully while Dok's eyes changed, and fired. The slug hit Dok just over the heart and pushed him backward away from the window of the car, hitting him like a club and sprawling him in the dusty street.

# FROM THE NICK CARTER
# KILLMASTER SERIES

AFGHAN INTERCEPT

THE ALGARVE AFFAIR

THE ANDROPOV FILE

THE ASSASSIN CONVENTION

ASSIGNMENT: RIO

THE BERLIN TARGET

BLACK SEA BLOODBATH

BLOOD OF THE FALCON

BLOOD RAID

BLOOD OF THE SCIMITAR

BLOODTRAIL TO MECCA

BLOOD ULTIMATUM

BOLIVIAN HEAT

THE BLUE ICE AFFAIR

THE BUDAPEST RUN

CARIBBEAN COUP

CIRCLE OF SCORPIONS

CODE NAME COBRA

COUNTDOWN TO ARMAGEDDON

CROSSFIRE RED

DAY OF THE ASSASSIN

THE DEADLY DIVA

THE DEATH DEALER

DEATH HAND PLAY

DEATH ISLAND

DEATH SQUAD

THE DEATH STAR AFFAIR

DEATHSTRIKE

DRAGONFIRE

THE DUBROVNIK MASSACRE

EAST OF HELL

THE EXECUTION EXCHANGE

HOLY WAR

INVITATION TO DEATH

KILLING GAMES

THE KILLING GROUND

THE KOREAN KILL

THE KREMLIN KILL

LAST FLIGHT TO MOSCOW

THE LAST SAMURAI

LETHAL PREY

THE MACAO MASSACRE

THE MASTER ASSASSIN

THE MAYAN CONNECTION

MERCENARY MOUNTAIN

NIGHT OF THE CONDOR

NIGHT OF THE WARHEADS

THE NORMANDY CODE

OPERATION PETROGRAD

OPERATION SHARKBITE

THE PARISIAN AFFAIR

THE POSEIDON TARGET

PRESSURE POINT

THE RANGOON MAN

THE REDOLMO AFFAIR

REICH FOUR

RETREAT FOR DEATH

THE SAMURAI KILL

SAN JUAN INFERNO

THE SATAN TRAP

SIGN OF THE COBRA

SLAUGHTER DAY

SPYKILLER

THE STRONTIUM CODE

THE SUICIDE SEAT

TARGET RED STAR

TERMS OF VENGEANCE

THE TERROR CODE

TERROR TIMES TWO

TIME CLOCK OF DEATH

TRIPLE CROSS

TUNNEL FOR TRAITORS

TURKISH BLOODBATH

THE VENGEANCE GAME

WAR FROM THE CLOUDS

WHITE DEATH

THE YUKON TARGET

ZERO-HOUR STRIKE FORCE

# THE KOREAN KILL

# KILL MASTER

# NICK CARTER

JOVE BOOKS, NEW YORK

"Nick Carter" is a registered trademark of The Condé Nast
Publications, Inc., registered in the United States Patent Office.

KILLMASTER #248: THE KOREAN KILL

A Jove Book / published by arrangement with
The Condé Nast Publications, Inc.

PRINTING HISTORY
Jove edition / April 1989

ISBN: 0-515-09983-X

Jove Books are published by The Berkley Publishing Group,
200 Madison Avenue, New York, New York 10016.
The name "JOVE" and the "J" logo
are trademarks belonging to Jove Publications, Inc.

PRINTED IN THE UNITED STATES OF AMERICA

10  9  8  7  6  5  4  3  2  1

*Dedicated to the men and women of the
Secret Services of the
United States of America*

# ONE

A small, one-column, two-inch story in the March 7 issue of the *Tokyo Sun* on page three:

A Japanese businessman, Ito Sukimoto, was stricken by a fatal heart attack in mid-flight on board JAL Flight 821 over the Sea of Japan. Flight 821 was en route from Seoul, Korea, to Tokyo International Airport. No foul play is suspected, but authorities are perplexed about a large sum of American and Canadian dollars found in a secret compartment of Mr. Sukimoto's luggage. It is said the amount found was in excess of three million dollars.

What the newspaper item didn't say—because it was never released—was the fact that the money was counterfeit.

# TWO

It was cold in Detroit, even for March, colder than a ten-dollar whore's heart. The kind of cold that threatened to crack your eyeballs, if you had the guts to open your eyes.

Lafayette Park was all ice, snow, and gloom, except around the candy-apple-red Corvette with the body half-in, half-out on the driver's side. In that section of the park there were lots of lights and lots of people inside and outside the wide orange plastic strips spread from tree to tree around the Corvette. Printed in large black block letters on the orange strips were the words CRIME SCENE.

Inside the orange strips were lots of flashing blue lights, uniforms, and bored faces.

Outside were the curious, most of them night people from the nearby Orleans section of bars, porno shops, strip joints, and hot-bed hotels along Lafayette Boulevard.

In the rear of the curious clutch of humanity, a four-door Ford rolled to the curb and two men, bored resignation on their faces, stepped out. They were dressed almost alike, dark topcoats over dark suits, white shirts, and rep ties. They both wore heavy solid black shoes.

The shorter of the two men was black. His name was Arnold Washington. He was thirty-one years old and had nine years in with the Detroit P.D. The whole nine years, except for his twelve weeks at the academy, had been in the Third Precinct.

The second man was white, and he towered by six inches over his partner. His name was Con Murrey. He, too, had nine years of police work, but the first three had been spent as a patrol officer in Grosse Pointe Shores where his family lived.

"Why," Murrey was often asked, "did you leave a cushy beat in Grosse Pointe to come down to slimeville?"

His answer usually went something like, "Hookers. I dig arresting hookers, and there ain't no local hookers in Grosse Pointe. They fly 'em all in from Paris."

Not too far from the truth.

Con Murrey was a cop because he liked action. And there was no action anywhere like there was in downtown Detroit. His old buddies just shook their heads when told of the transfer. Then they heard he had *requested* the Third.

"The Third? Christ, I've heard about the Third. They say you do your whole twenty with your dick in one hand and your Colt in the other. You're always shootin' somethin' in the Third!"

Not too far from the truth.

As the two detectives neared the outer ring of onlookers, a tall black in a long leather coat, white shoes, and a purple hat turned to one of the two women by his side.

"We is all saved from the bad peoples now, ladies," he grinned, showing gold caps to match the gold chains around his neck. "Here come the plainclothes pigs!"

Arnold Washington heard the comment, and just happened to come down with his size ten on the instep of the pimp's right foot. The man howled in pain and began jumping on his left foot.

"What the fuck, man . . ."

"I am sorry, sir," Washington said, not a trace of black street-speak in his voice. "An accident."

"Accident, shit, motherfucker!"

"Would you like to file a complaint, sir?"

"You bet your Uncle-Tom ass I—"

Suddenly, Con Murrey stepped between them until he was looking straight down at the pimp. His voice, when he spoke, was a molasses whisper. "My partner is a black man. He doesn't like to pound on a brother. Me, I don't give a shit. I like to pound on everybody. You want to step over in those trees? I'll take your complaint."

The pimp, helped by his two lady friends, hobbled hurriedly away. The two detectives strolled through the crowd that parted before them.

Just inside the barricades they were met by Officer Jo Sterne.

Sterne, at twenty-six, was a four-year vet. She wore her long, light-brown hair in a clip at the nape of her neck. Her profile and proportions echoed a classical beauty, which could make her, in the eyes of the average male chauvinist, very much out of place in a police uniform.

That is, until you stared at the ice in her blue eyes. The eyes told you that every inch of her attractive five-eight frame was a cop.

Washington grinned. "Sterne, for a white girl, you're sexy."

"I know."

"What've we got?" Murrey asked.

"Asian male, about twenty-five, gunshot. It looks like two slugs. M.E.'s working on him now."

"You find him?"

"No, that one over there by the tree did."

By the tree was a lanky, bearded bum in a tattered raincoat, scuffed cowboy boots, baggy pants, and a shirt that two gallons of bleach wouldn't make white again. A bored uniformed officer was holding him up at arm's length to avoid the smell of his breath.

Sterne flipped open her notebook. "Name's Herman Wyman. He's called Hinky. Says he lives at the Chester ... sometimes."

"I know the place," Washington offered. "A fleabag up on Adelaide."

"Right."

"Jeez, I can smell him from here," Murrey said, nostrils twitching.

"It's wearing off a little," Sterne replied. "He was knee-walking when I got here."

"Did he call it in?"

"No. I was going by in my mobile. He ran out and flagged me down. That was at two-oh-five."

Murrey checked his watch. It was three-twenty.

"Where's the beef?"

The speaker was Jerry Fogerty, a photographer who worked free-lance for the department. He was a hundred and forty pounds of skeleton on a six-four frame. Because of his droopy eyes and hang-dog face, he always looked as if he were asleep. There were two cameras slung around his neck and another at his side in his right hand.

"This way," Sterne said, and led them toward the car.

The Corvette was a T-top, last year's model, and it had all the trimmings, inside and out.

The body was across the seat, its arms flung out. One

leg was twisted under the other. A leather jacket was folded neatly on the passenger seat. The body wore a pair of tan slacks, brown loafers, and a beige sweater over a white shirt. The bloody sweater had dried to a wad of dark stain.

As they approached, the medical examiner, Harvey Edelman, a paunchy little man with a grim face and a halo of gray hair around a bald pate, stood up. He turned to the two police lab officers and nodded.

"It's all yours."

The lab boys and Jerry Fogerty went to work.

Con Murrey took a sweeping, hard look and shook hands with Harvey Edelman. "What've we got?"

"We got a stiff, of course," he replied, shifting the butt of a ragged cigar from one side of his mouth to the other. "He's been a stiff for about two and a half hours . . ."

"That would make the time of death about one o'clock?"

Edelman nodded. "He got to be a stiff because he caught two slugs from the rear. One severed his spine at the base of the neck, the other rattled around inside his skull until it entered his brain. I'll know more for sure when I cut him open."

"What caliber?" Washington asked.

"Shit, you know better than to ask that 'til I dig 'em out."

"Okay, okay. What do you guess?"

"Big, not too big, like a Mag. Probably a forty-five. Here's the shit from his pockets. Don't worry about prints. I don't think any of it was disturbed."

The medical examiner held up a clear plastic bag. Murrey took it and signed the evidence receipt.

"Any more questions? It's a busy night—I got another one up on Grover."

"How soon can we get the report?" Murrey asked.

"Christ, when I get it done." Edelman strolled away.

Murrey shook his head and turned back to the body. "Nice car, nice clothes. The shoes are Gucci, aren't they?"

"I'd say so," Washington agreed. "What the hell was he doin' down here after midnight?"

"Maybe buying some pussy," Jo Sterne offered. The two men looked at her with wide eyes. She shrugged. "I thought I'd say it before you did. That's what was on your mind, wasn't it?"

"Sergeant Murrey. . ."

It was one of the lab boys on the passenger side of the car. Murrey and Washington walked around. The man had the center console open. Inside were a bunch of cassette tapes, and between the man's thumb and index finger was a U.S. Army-issue Colt .45.

"Been fired?" Murrey asked.

"No. It looks like he was going for this, though, when he bought it."

"It does at that," Washington said.

"And look here."

The two detectives leaned forward. Where the serial number should have been on the gun, there was only blotched metal.

"Looks like an acid job," Washington murmured.

"Yeah. What's a nice Japanese kid doing with a hot gun?" Murrey wondered. "Special messenger it down to the lab. It's a sloppy job. Maybe a few numbers can be brought back."

"Yes, sir."

They moved to the back of the car and unloaded the plastic bag. Inside was a wallet, one five-dollar bill, a parking receipt, two quarters, four nickels, a penny, a pack of Juicy Fruit gum, a confirmation slip for two nights at the

Mandarin Palace Hotel in Kowloon, and an airline ticket for that evening to San Francisco with a continuing flight to Hong Kong.

"Traveled light," Washington commented.

"Maybe not."

Murrey started emptying the wallet, spreading the bills across the hood of the car.

"Sheeeeiit." Washington counted $3,740 in hundreds, fifties, and twenties. "So much for robbery as the motive."

"Unless the robber was an idiot," Murrey said. He held a driver's license up to the light. "Our boy is Toby Sukimoto, age twenty-seven, Asian male, five-six, one-forty. He lives at Twenty-one-oh-seven Queens Road, Windsor."

Washington glanced down. "Plates on the Vette are Michigan."

"Check the registration," Murrey said, leafing through the rest of the cards in the wallet.

Washington got it from the glove compartment and returned. "Vette's registered to Blue Chip Enterprises, One-fourteen Wesley Lane. That's over in Inkster."

"Ever heard of 'em?" Murrey asked.

"Vaguely," Washington said. "I think they deal in some kind of computer parts."

Jerry Fogerty slouched toward them. "That's it for the meat. Got the car, got all the shit. Anything else?"

Murrey was about to reply, when Officer Sterne came jogging their way.

"Sergeant . . ."

"Yeah?"

"They found a piece, there, about a hundred yards into the trees."

"What is it?"

"An Army-issue forty-five," she replied.

All of them moved into the trees. A uniformed officer

knelt beside a bush, thick with snow. The beam from his six-cell flash was on the automatic under the bush.

"Jerry, get a shot."

Three flashbulbs later, Washington reached in with his pen, hooked it, and brought it out. He sniffed the barrel. "It's been fired, recently. And look . . ."

"Acid, just like the one in the Vette," Murrey said. "Send it to the lab boys. Let's talk to Hinky."

"You guys don't believe me, do ya."

Con Murrey looked at the slovenly figure. Wyman was nervous, and beneath his shaggy hair, worry pinched his brows. He looked as if he were trying to vomit, but nothing would come up but air.

"Any reason we shouldn't?" Murrey asked.

"No! But . . . I mean . . . all these questions. Shit, I was just crossin' through the park."

Washington stepped in closer to the drunk. Even though the man's smell hit his nostrils like a truck, he managed not to wince. He even smiled. "Don't worry about my partner. He's not really a hard-ass. Just gotta ask questions is all. Understand?"

"Sure . . . sure, Officer, I unnerstan'."

"Good. What were you doing in the park?"

"I had a pint, Old Crow . . . good stuff."

"And you didn't want to share it with anybody," Murrey said.

"Tha's right. Lotta criminal types 'round here, steal a man's teeth let alone his ration."

Washington nodded and shifted his weight from one tired leg to the other. "We understand that, Mr. Wyman. We just want to get everything down now so we don't have to dig you up later—"

Murrey interrupted. "What time did you find the deceased?"

"How the fuck do I know? Ain't had a watch in years." His watery eyes flickered to the two men. "Shouldn'ta got involved. You think I did it."

"We don't know who did it," Murrey said, "yet."

"Did you pass anybody before you got to the car?"

"Nah . . . I dunno . . . I'd had a belt or two."

One of the two men in white from the morgue wagon appeared at Murrey's shoulder. "They're all done. Can we load?"

"Yeah, go ahead," Murrey replied, turning back to the old man. "Did you touch anything?"

"Nah, hell no. I seen the guy there. I says, 'Hey, buddy, you okay?' Ain't no answer. I go up a little closer. That's when I see the blood."

"Then you ran back out to the street?"

"Yeah, that's right."

"And saw Officer Sterne cruising."

The man cackled. "Yeah, I saw this broad cruising and I tell her there's a dead guy. Can I go now? Shouldn'ta got involved. Hell, I'm just a homeless guy likes a drink now and then . . ."

"Are you staying at the Chester, sir?" Washington asked.

The bleary, bloodshot eyes looked up into the black face. "When I got the seven bucks for the room."

"Just need to know in case we have to ask you a few more questions," Murrey said.

"Sure, sure. Hey . . . ya know I used ta be an accountant?"

Washington nodded. "You can go."

"Can I have my pint back?"

Murrey glanced at the nearby officer. He held up a pint

of Old Crow with about two fingers in the bottom. He nodded, and the two detectives moved back toward the Corvette.

"Think he might have seen somebody?" Washington asked.

"Could have. He acts like it. Could be too afraid to say, or he might have been too drunk to see anything."

They met Sterne at the Vette. "The grid's been gone over twice. You gonna want me for anything else? My shift's due off in an hour."

"No, go ahead, thanks," Murrey replied. "No sense wasting the overtime."

Sterne moved off toward her black and white.

Only half aware of the retreating officer, Murrey let his mind play over the scene again, trying to see it from the angle of the victim. Then from that of the killer. Night. Over there, beyond the straggling line of officers working their way back toward the cars, a few distant lights from Lafayette Boulevard. A car or two heard in the distance, passing across the dim haze of city lights. That's what the victim would have seen: the glare of Detroit's lights against the sky, and in front of that, the killer.

"What you thinkin'?" Washington asked. "A mob hit?"

Murrey pursed his lips. "Two in the back of the head. It would look like it, wouldn't it. But that throws something else on the table. What's a nice clean-cut kid doing on a first-name basis with the mob?"

Washington grinned. Their minds were already working in tandem.

Sukimoto had obviously gotten out of the car to talk to his killer. He knew him.

"Let's go in," Murrey said. "We'll start piecing it together over coffee."

Both men headed for their unmarked unit.

In the next two hours, they would find out that the two .45 automatics were part of an arms shipment hijacked outside Pusan, Korea, in 1951.

They would also learn that Blue Chip Enterprises was under secret investigation by the FBI for illegal trading in electronics parts to a foreign power.


Hinky Wyman hurried down the alley clutching the thin briefcase to his chest as if he were drowning and it was his life preserver.

He had lied to the police, of course. He had seen the hit from his hiding place in the trees. The two Chinks or Japs or whatever they were had been arguing. Then the one had dived into the car and the other one just blew him away.

Then the killer had grabbed the briefcase and started to run. He had paused long enough to throw the gun into the woods and then had taken off again. Hinky had followed him to a black motorcycle and watched him stuff the briefcase into a saddlebag.

It was then that the killer looked up and spotted Hinky. The little Asian was fast, but Hinky had been drinking and sleeping it off in the park for years. He knew every tree, every path, and every place to hide.

He eluded the killer and doubled back to the motorcycle. He grabbed the briefcase and unzipped it as he ran.

"Damn . . . oh damn, damn, damn!"

Inside the briefcase Hinky saw money. Stacks and stacks of hundred-dollar-bill money. He also saw the black-clad motorcycle rider trying to cut him off at the edge of the park.

That was when he'd stuffed the briefcase into the rear end of his pants and ran toward the cruising police car. The motorcycle man got the message, cut away from Hinky, and headed for his bike.

Now Hinky was headed for the bus station. He would take the first bus out to anywhere and then get another headed for Florida.

Florida.

It was Hinky's dream. With all those hundreds he could have all the booze and hot sands his wracked old body could handle.

At first it was only a shadow, several yards ahead where the alley came to a facing wall and took an abrupt turn to the right.

The shadow turned into the figure of a man, a man dressed all in black. Too late, Hinky saw the helmet.

"Give me the case, old man."

Hinky froze and the figure advanced.

*What the hell*, Hinky thought, *he doesn't have his gun. I saw him throw it into the woods. And, hell, he's just a little shit, not more than five-five.*

Hinky might be drunk, but he was big and still strong.

"Don't be a fool, old man. All I want is the case."

Hinky went for him. But he never reached him.

Suddenly the little man was in the air, the spread-eagle of his legs plummeting toward Hinky's head. The old man tried to duck, but he didn't move fast enough. The boots caught him in the chest and he was on the ground.

The side of a hand connected with Hinky's nose, breaking it. The briefcase was torn from his hands. He reached up and managed to slam the other man on the side of the head.

"Stupid old man."

Hinky felt two powerful thumbs on each side of his Adam's apple. He could get no breath. His lungs were exploding and all he could see before his eyes was red, as if he were looking straight into the sun.

Then the orb of hot light and pain spiraled away into darkness.

# THREE

## *March 12*

Nick Carter paused at the entrance to Upper Lascar Row, dug a handkerchief from his pocket and mopped the perspiration from his face.

In front of him were the steep ladder streets that sprawled across Hong Kong's immense Thieves Market.

Six hours earlier he had made the morning rendezvous on Hong Kong's seaward shore. The place was called Milady's. It was a little tea shop among the bathers' striped tent-cabanas and colorful beach umbrellas.

He had waited two hours, and no Sukimoto.

Now he was hitting the fallback.

He lit a cigarette and went over in his mind the tape of the first conversation and the content of his own, personal telephone call to Toby Sukimoto.

The first, taped, conversation had been to the FBI in Washington:

"My name is Toby Sukimoto. My father was Ito Sukimoto. My father is dead. For this reason I want to cleanse his soul and wipe a blot from our family name. I have information for your intelligence service about the flood of counterfeit money coming from the Far East. And also I have proof of military electronic secrets and components being sold to Communist countries.

"Please contact me at 555-7414 in Windsor, Ontario, in five hours' time."

Within an hour the information had been passed to the CIA, but because an AXE agent had already been killed in the investigation the caller spoke of, the responsibility had been kicked along to Dupont Circle and Nick Carter.

At the precise hour, Carter had returned the call.

"My name is Nick Carter. I am connected to a special agency with the State Department and returning an earlier call from Toby Sukimoto."

"I am Sukimoto. I have all the proof and names you need to bring down Dr. Kwon."

"Dr. Kwon?"

"It is Dr. Kwon who is responsible for everything I mentioned earlier."

"How can we make contact?" Carter had asked.

The instructions were simple and to the point. In three days' time, at nine o'clock on the morning of March 12, Carter, wearing a white jogging suit and carrying a Spaulding tennis racket, would have morning tea at Milady's.

If in two hours' time Sukimoto had not made contact, Carter was to return to his hotel until three in the afternoon. At that time he was to go to the shop of Sen Lo, an antiques dealer in the Thieves Market.

An elaborate identification code was given to Carter to make himself known to the antiques dealer. Sen Lo would tell Carter where to make the second meet.

"Why Hong Kong?"

"Because, Mr. Carter, once I give you this information I

must run and run very fast. Hong Kong is a very good place to run from."

The Killmaster found the shop on the second tier of steps in the market.

Inside, it was small, dark, crowded with junk, and reeking of incense. A huge stick burned in the belly of a porcelain Buddha.

Behind the Buddha, in a carved teak armchair, sat a grossly fat man with a shaved head. His pig eyes were nearly lost in the fat of his cheeks, and the palm leaf fan he waved did nothing to stop the sweat that poured from his face.

Two women with sharp English accents were trying, vainly it would seem, to bargain with the fat man for a Chinese lion of oxidized bronze. The women could not persuade the shopkeeper to name a price for it.

They offered him fifty dollars as an opening. He shook his head without interrupting the rhythm of the fan. Fifty dollars? No. A hundred dollars? Still no. How much, then? What was he asking for it?

"Not ask," he said. "Not foah sale. Thank you. Goodbye."

"But what kind of a shop *is* this?" one of the ladies asked, annoyed. "Whoever heard of an antiques dealer who wouldn't sell an antique? Just name me a price, any price . . ."

"Oh, come along, Alice," the other said. "You're just wasting our time. There are lots of other places to look at."

"But I can't *understand* it," Alice protested. "It just doesn't make sense to me. If the man's in business . . ."

The woman was still complaining as she and her companion joined the never-ending flow of people on the street outside.

"I am interested in jade," Carter said, lighting a cigarette.

"All kinds of jade . . . good jade, bad jade. What kind of jade you look for?"

The pig eyes never wavered in their intensity. They were as cold, distrustful, and sharp as the rest of him was gross, fat, and sweaty.

Carter wondered what kind of a character Toby Sukimoto was if Sen Lo was one of his friends.

"I'm interested in a jade Buddha, twelfth century."

The fan did not alter its slow rhythm, although the pig eyes behind it showed a spark of interest. "Very old, not cheap."

Carter took the money clip from his pocket, extracted two bills, each a thousand Hong Kong dollars, and put them where the Chinese could reach them. He didn't reach. But he looked.

"The piece I want is Siang Ju, one of the one hundred made for the courtesan Po Fang Du."

A fat hand scraped the money into a drawer. "You have papers, passport?"

Carter flashed his diplomatic passport and his State Department Special Agent credentials card. The pig eyes narrowed even more and the fat lips moved, spelling out the letters.

"You are Nicholas Carter?"

"That's right."

"Tonight you take *wallah-wallah* to whorehouse junks in Causeway Bay. Junk you want is *Mandarin Joy*. You catch girl named Po Lin. She tell you rest. Goo-bye."

"Will this Po Lin . . . ?"

Carter knew it was useless. He moved back into the foot traffic of Upper Lascar Row. At the first opportunity, he turned left and ran up two levels. The dirt and the noise increased as he climbed. There was the constant clatter of wooden wheels on the cobbles, quacks of crated ducks on their way to market, and the shouts of porters on heavily loaded bicycles clearing a way for themselves.

He guessed at a narrow alley between two shops and darted into it. The guess was right. He was directly above and across from the antiques shop.

The traffic was still the same, always in movement in front of the shop. No one loitered or showed any sign of interest in what might be going on inside.

Carter waited fifteen minutes before he was rewarded.

There were two of them, both in conservative dark lightweight suits. Even at such a distance Carter could tell that they were not Chinese; they were Japanese, perhaps, or Korean.

He watched until he was sure they were headed for Hennessy Road, then sprinted up the levels on his parallel road.

He spotted a taxi and waved it down.

"Okay, where go?"

"Wait," Carter said, and dropped a Hong Kong hundred on the front seat.

"Wait as long as you want, buddy," the cabbie said with a toothy grin.

It wasn't a long wait. The pair emerged on Hennessy Road and walked directly to a black Mercedes limousine with a Chinese driver.

"Follow that limousine at a distance," Carter murmured.

"What you, man . . . spy?"

"Jealous husband."

"Ho, ho, man, sure enough!"

The limo hit Nathan Road and left the central district. In no time they were on the exposed eastern shore riding the coastal road above wide sandy beaches. Huge rollers off the open ocean boomed and broke below the cliffs.

"Turn into big house drive, boss."

"I see," Carter said. "Stop here."

The house was on the crest of one of the higher hills overlooking the ocean. Vast green lawns and gardens surrounded it, and a gravel driveway wound down to a pair of huge iron gates.

The limo paused for only a few seconds. The gates opened and it drove through.

Carter checked a street sign and then tapped the driver on the shoulder. "Drive on!"

All the big houses in the area had names rather than numbers. This one was Sea Breeze.

"Where to now, boss?"

"The Peak," Carter said.

The taxi driver left him at the foot of the cable car, and Carter rode it up to the Peak where wealthy *taipans* or businessmen from all over the world maintained houses.

The one Carter wanted was one of the largest, a sprawling, three-story affair behind a high brick wall. The gates were open, and as Carter walked up the drive he could hear a battle of music, one blast coming from the pool and patio, the other from the interior of the house.

The reason for the music and the laughter, Carter knew, was one of the longest-running parties in Southeast Asia.

The owner of the house was Lord Something-or-Other's playboy son. He and his then mistress had started the party approximately six months earlier. After about a month, the young lord had gone on to greener pastures. The mistress was left behind, but the party hadn't stopped.

Now hardly anyone remembered the young lord's name, and nobody cared. There was no shortage of food or drink, and the credit was evidently bottomless. The pretty people had heard about the party in Tokyo, San Francisco, Gstaad, or Monte Carlo, and just dropped by . . . and stayed.

The party drew its share of have-nots who came to live in unaccustomed luxury off the haves. They, too, brought trade goods, mostly bodies. Sleek, curved, responsive girl-bodies for the males, and lean, snake-hipped, tanned boys for the golden ladies who wanted such. And boy-man or girl-woman for those inclined that way.

There were ten bedrooms and fifteen full baths, several of them big enough to double as playpens for a pet porpoise, in case anything like that happened. Stranger creatures had been on the guest list, including a tortoise big enough to ride on, and an overly friendly boa constrictor.

There were periods when the party could have passed for an international trade fair of dope dealers. Foreign agents came and went and did their deals and told each other lies about Lisbon and Singapore and Vienna and Zurich in the old days.

The door keys had been lost as long as the absentee host, and very few visitors drew attention when they walked through the wide-open carved mahogany portals.

One of the agents who had arrived four months earlier was a broad-shouldered, golden-haired giant named Rodney Coolidge. He had gone to all the right schools and knew all the right people. He also fit the image of the world-weary, roving playboy.

Coolidge was also a crack MI6 agent, and had gleaned some extremely valuable information in the four months in the house.

A request from AXE for Coolidge's help was granted at once, right down to Carter moving in.

Inside, Carter moved through milling people. They all seemed to wear a standard uniform: bikinis for females, with skimpy, diaphanous beach jackets, even if far from the sands. For males, swim trunks, sometimes with a sportshirt, was the uniform of the day. Evenings, a little more: jeans were considered formal attire. Out of regard for the sun, both sexes wore straw hats with wide brims. Shoulder bags were practical in a society without pockets, and were universally carried.

Since Carter had spent only one night in the place, he knew very few of the guests. As he pushed through a dozen or so in the vast living room, he spotted the blonde with the black eye who had moved into his bed the previous night.

She was young, maybe twenty-five, with a man of sun-gold hair. Slender, but with nice bumps and curves and notable legs. Her hair was sun-bleached to a straw color, somewhat in disarray, with a little curl to the ends. Her face was pretty enough, with an aristocratic nose, high cheekbones, and wide, sensuous lips. The eye that was not blackened and puffed shut was cornflower blue.

"Vera . . . ?"

"Hi! Come home to roost?"

"I need Coolidge."

"Rodney? I don't think he's up yet."

Carter headed for the stairs. On the third floor, he pushed through the door of the master bedroom. It was a huge, rich room, the far wall entirely glass which opened onto the terrace and bay beyond.

Coolidge was on his belly, naked, on the bed. Astride him, also naked, was the young lord's ex-mistress. While she rubbed his buttocks with her buttocks, she was also applying suntan lotion to his back.

"Nick, old sod!" Coolidge cackled when he spotted Carter. "Just getting ready for a little sun. Put on a pair of trunks and join us. Or *don't* put on a pair of trunks and join us!"

"You had lunch yet?"

"No."

"Then let's have some lunch and talk."

Coolidge nodded. "Sure. Magda, fetch us a pitcher of Bloody Marys, will you, old girl?"

The sleepy-eyed ex-mistress rolled off the bed and wiggled from the room, still naked. Coolidge grabbed a pair of swim trunks and scrambled into them. Both men moved onto the balcony and settled into rattan chairs.

"How did it go?"

"It went," Carter murmured, "and that was about all."

He told the Englishman about the fat antiques dealer and the two men in dark suits.

"Sounds like a bloody trap to me," Coolidge growled.

Carter nodded. "But why?"

"Maybe they figure this Sukimoto had told you more on the phone than he did."

Magda returned with two glasses and a pitcher of Bloody Marys.

"You're not joining us, luv?" Coolidge asked.

She shrugged her lovely bare shoulders. "Business bores me, this place bores me, life bores me. I'm going to go drown in the swimming pool."

"You do that, luv."

When she was gone, Carter spoke again. "No matter what it is . . . a scam, a trap . . . I've got to go."

"And you need a backup?"

"I'd like one, if you can tear yourself away from all this for an evening."

Coolidge chuckled. "Hey, it's about time I exercised some other muscles."

"A couple of other things. There's a place on the bluff road, on the open side of the island. I'd like to know who owns it. I mean, *really* owns it. Also, they have a couple of houseguests, maybe more."

"The dark suits?"

Carter nodded. "Names, if possible. I think they're Japanese or Korean."

"Shouldn't be too difficult. I'll get right on it. What time do we party tonight?"

"I'll head out to the junk around ten," Carter replied. "I'd like to have you already there, about eight."

"Will do," Coolidge said, nodding, filling the glasses from the pitcher. He gestured to the house. "You hanging around here?"

"Yeah. I think I'll have a swim, a shower, and a little shut-eye. It could be one hell of a long night."

He had just shifted the water from icy cold to warm, when the shower door slid open.

It was Vera. "Hi."

"Hi yourself," Carter said.

"Want a little yin and yang?"

Carter couldn't help but laugh. Vera wasn't too bright, but she had one hell of a carnal appetite and a great sense of humor. All in all, it wasn't a bad combination.

"Why not," he replied, and grinned. "C'mere."

He caught her by the hips and lifted her into the shower. The black-and-blue eye and the cornflower-blue eye looked him over greedily. There was no question she was stoned.

She moved into him and rolled her belly upward over his splayed legs. Moaning, she stood while he knelt and slid forward on the wet floor. His lips ran over her silky inner thighs, leaving a trail of moisture on the smooth skin and her tingling nerve ends.

She stroked his hair as she rotated her hips against his mouth, making herself respond to the darting pressure of his expert tongue.

"Oh, God, that's good," she whimpered. "I got myself all worked up this afternoon just dreaming about last night."

He leaned back and gazed up into her passion-filled face. He slid his hands up the backs of her legs and slowly worked his way upward until he cupped her firm buttocks. As his hands moved, her body shook with the pleasure she was anticipating.

She urged his lips back to her firm, quivering thighs and rammed herself forward in need.

Carter kissed her gently and then pulled his head back and stood up. Vera put her arms around his torso and pulled his body tightly to hers.

"Take it easy," he murmured, "you'll be ready too soon."

"Oh, God, I'm ready now!" she cried.

He could sense the urgency in her body. His nostrils filled with the smell of her. His hands worked between her thighs, feeling the desire flow through her. His eyes roamed her body, across her heaving belly, to the jutting, firm mounds of her breasts. The rose-tipped flesh jiggled and bounced provocatively as she moved. Her nipples were rock-hard, and they throbbed with passion.

Her hands went up to her breasts. She lifted them in her palms and smiled into his eyes.

Carter watched with fascination as she held herself out in offering to him, her thumbs strumming her nipples. Under her manipulations, her breasts looked fuller. Carter found his breathing becoming labored with added desire and lust as he watched them swell.

He felt he should say something, to tell her how much he enjoyed her body, but when he tried to speak, he found his throat dry. His eyes moved up and found hers. He knew then that no words were necessary; he could see approval in her eyes.

"Enough is enough," he growled.

He picked her up and, soaking wet, carried her to the bed. He moved his body between her thighs, and she took over.

His breathing became heavier as his hips tried to keep a steady pace against the writhing, insanely bucking body. He was stretched tight. His nerve ends were right on the edge. It was glorious and he wanted to make it last as long as he could.

It was fast, maybe too fast, but she seemed to get as much thrill out of the results as he.

He rolled to her side and, in seconds, felt a drowsy peace overtake him.

"Are you rich?"

"Huh?" he said, struggling against the drowsiness. Her voice seemed to come from a well.

"Do you have a lot of money?"

"Not a sou. Been broke all my life."

"Oh. Well, I guess it's good that you're too old for me, then."

Carter squinted his eyes, trying to focus on her corn-flower-blue one. "How's that?"

She shrugged, making her breasts jiggle delightfully. "Because I don't really want to fall in love with an older man, but if I did, he would have to have a lot of money.

And since you don't have any money, I guess there's no way I'll fall in love with you."

"Vera . . ."

"Huh?"

"Nighty-night."

Just in case, he buried her face in his chest to discourage any more deep and brilliant forays into philosophy.

# FOUR

It was a hot night, windless and clear, as Carter rode the cable car down from the Peak to the central section of the city.

Hong Kong's nighttime blaze of neon was in full glory against the dark sky. The island side of the harbor, with its skyscraper hotels, banks, and office buildings, reflected the top-to-bottom illumination of floodlighting. Beyond, the harbor was full of shipping, most of it with working lights on, and elements of the Seventh Fleet anchored in Causeway Bay wore full nautical dress. So did several British naval vessels anchored in the roadstead, all of them strung with runners and ribbons of light from masthead to masthead, stem to stern, outlines of ships drawn in incandescence against dark water on which their reflections gleamed almost as brilliantly upside down.

At the bottom he took a cab to the harbor. He was scarcely out of the cab when the *wallah-wallah*, or water taxi, drivers descended. Carter chose the youngest of them, a mother who looked about fourteen with a baby strapped to her back, and allowed her to lead him to her tiny craft.

"Where you go?"

"Causeway junk line."

"You want restaurant or whorehouse?"

"The *Mandarin Joy*."

"Good show. Hang on."

The *wallah-wallah*'s single-stroke engine started a wheezy thump, and the teen-age mother steered for Causeway Bay and the floating boat colony beyond its breakwater.

As they putt-putted across the still water, the air became heavy with the smell of joss, fish, rank sea-growth clinging to the hulls of a thousand other *wallah-wallahs*, sampans, junks, and patched-up floating boxes where untold thousands of people were born, lived, reproduced, and died.

The hulks of the floating community were jampacked so closely together in their anchorage that the boat people could clamber from vessel to vessel, aided now and then by a plank footbridge, like agile goats.

Between and among the anchored hulks were lanes left open for boat traffic and trade. They were like streets, with floating shops, stores, eating houses, teahouses, brothels, market boats, and joss temples lining their routes.

"There *Mandarin Joy*."

It was nearly the largest of the moored junks, brightly painted and lit from stem to stern with gaily colored lights.

Carter tipped the *wallah-wallah* girl heavily and climbed over the side. The doors to the main salon were drawn wide so that the visitor could walk right down from the deck into the room.

A bar lined the inner wall, couches of cheap red vinyl were battened to the fore and aft bulkheads, and easy chairs with small tables took up the rest of the room.

A few single Chinese men were at the bar. There were three tables of American sailors drinking, and about twenty

Chinese doll hostesses in Western-style evening gowns circulating.

Carter couldn't spot Rodney Coolidge. He did spot two hundred pounds of giggling Chinese madam in a red tent as she moved from man to man promoting business.

Carter moved to the bar and ordered a scotch, knowing that she would get to him sooner or later.

She arrived with the drink.

"Hi-lo, baybee, drink on house. You American and you too old to be sailor boy, so I buy you drink, make you feel good, you spend more money. In Chinese I am Ho Ling Ahn. In American I am Howling Annie. What kind girl you like?"

All this was said in one breath.

"A friend of mine suggested Po Lin."

"Ah, damn good choice, best girl in Hong Kong. You and your friend must be rich."

"How rich?"

"For Po Lin? Probably three hundred Hong Kong dollar rich."

Carter smiled. "Does the wedding come with that price?"

She howled and slapped Carter's thigh. "You smart-ass. Hokay, two hundred Hong Kong dollar, and I throw in bath. Hey, inflation very bad here."

"I think you're a Chinese thief, but it's a deal."

"Hokay, come on!"

She led the way through the innards of the big junk to a beautifully appointed bedroom.

"You take off clothes. I get Po Lin."

She waddled out, and Carter checked the closets and the bath. Just in case he did have to disrobe, he removed his shoulder rig and the chamois sheath strapped to his right forearm. In one was his 9mm Luger, in the other a deadly stiletto. He hid them in an overhead rack behind a pile of towels.

He was just pulling on his jacket when the door opened and a young, round-faced girl in a loosely belted robe bounced into the room. Without a word she started removing Carter's clothes.

"Hey, are you Po Lin?"

"Oh, yes. How come you so slow?"

"Do you know San Lo—"

"No talk. Bath now."

He had little choice, so he let her lead him into the bath. She took the wooden top from the tub and the room immediately filled with steam.

"In!"

When he was too slow, she pushed him down into the water. She shrugged out of the robe and, with her bare breasts bouncing freely, scrubbed him from chin to ankle.

"There, clean. You dry, come into bedroom."

Carter stepped from the tub beet red. She draped a huge towel around him and left, closing the door behind her.

He quickly patted himself dry, wound the towel around his middle, and stepped into the bedroom. He was barely through the door when he froze.

The cigarette smoke that warned him came from across the dim room.

"My, Po Lin, how you've changed."

She crushed out the cigarette and stood, moving farther into the light away from the bed.

She was tall, with long legs clad in short black boots and dark pants, over which she wore an apple-green suede jacket that was not expensive but of good cut and taste. In the light, her hair glittered like coal, and it hung to her shoulders in a sleek soft fall. Her eyes were a deep brown and sloed, but the rest of her face was Western aristocrat.

Her upright bearing made Carter think of medieval ladies who defended the castle when their lord was off to the wars.

"Po Lin, like the rest of this, was a necessary subterfuge, Mr. Carter. We had to make sure you were not followed after contacting Sen Lo. Also, you had to be easily parted from your arms."

Carter reached above him and checked the rack. The Luger and the stiletto were gone.

"Well, since I'm not getting laid, do you mind if I get dressed?"

"Please do."

He waited a few seconds, and when she didn't turn around he shrugged and started pulling on his clothes. "You mentioned 'we'?"

"My name is Kim Li."

"You're not Chinese."

"No, I am Korean."

Carter sat to pull on his shoes. "You're not all Korean, either."

"No, my father was Australian, part of the U.N. peace-keeping force. I never knew him."

Carter stood, pulled on his jacket, and moved to stand in front of her. "All right, Kim Li, what the hell is going on?"

"My people wish to talk to you."

"And just who the hell are your people?"

"I am sorry, but I cannot tell you that right now."

Carter raised his hand and ran a finger down the side of her soft throat. Slowly, he pressed his thumb to her carotid artery and tightened his grip.

"I could kill you."

"I am sure you could," she replied calmly. "But if you do, you will learn nothing more about Toby Sukimoto."

That did it. She had said the magic words. At this point he had nothing to lose by going along with her.

"Okay, lady, right now the cards are all yours. Lead the way."

There was a second door in the panels beside the bath that he hadn't seen. Through it was a murky passageway that she lit with a pencil flashlight. It came out in a large galley that smelled of fried fish and sour plumbing. The galley was empty.

She pulled up a trap in the deck. "These stairs lead to a platform off the stern. I have a motor launch waiting. It is impossible to see from the shore or the other junks."

Carter looked down at the blackness, and hesitated.

"If you are thinking of your MI6 friend, Mr. Coolidge, he is asleep and has been for some time in the bedroom beside the one we have just left. He will be well taken care of."

"You think of everything, don't you," Carter growled.

"Everything. Please follow me."

He waited for her head to disappear then started down the ladder into the inky blackness himself.


The launch glided into a waterway underneath a rotting warehouse.

"Follow me, please."

She led him up three winding flights of iron stairway to a courtyard. It was cobbled, dark, and shiny with water that dripped from somewhere overhead. The area was crammed with empty boxes and crates. They squeezed through a passage no wider than Carter's shoulders, and came out onto the street about thirty feet away from the building entrance. A black car was drawn up in front of it.

Halfway to the car, Carter recognized the Mercedes limousine he had followed that afternoon.

"This place we're going," he said, "it wouldn't be called the Sea Breeze, would it?"

She smiled, for the first time since he had met her. "It is. The same house you followed my two friends to this afternoon."

Carter settled back in the seat.

*What a nice way,* he mused, *of informing me I had a tail all along and hadn't spotted it.*

The big car came to a halt, and they stepped out into the night air. The woman led him up the steps to the massive, iron-studded door. She knocked, using a cast-iron knocker that Carter noticed was made in the shape of a Buddha.

After a moment the door was swung back, and Carter faced a huge Asian. He wore a butler's livery, tails with a starched white collar. He wasn't terribly tall, perhaps six-two, but his shoulders were massive, blocking the doorway, and his body was stocky and powerful.

She spoke to the man in whispered Korean. He grunted a reply and, with a flourish, turned and led them inside.

He moved gracefully for such a big man, Carter thought. Then he passed under a light and Carter saw that he had no hands, only steel hooks protruding from his sleeves.

"He was caught above the Parallel a few years ago," the woman said, noting the look on Carter's face. "North Korean soldiers cut off his hands and sent him back."

The rooms and halls were large and decorated like the inside of a Chinese temple from a bygone era.

They followed him down endless passageways until they came at last to a long open room. Once it had been a dining hall or ballroom; the ceiling was high and elaborately carved and inlaid.

At the far end was a heavy, ancient desk. Behind it, in a

high-backed leather chair, sat a man, writing. He looked up and smiled as they entered.

The face that had once been handsome was now leathery with deep wrinkles. The color had almost totally gone from his features. The flesh was thinning and the skull had begun to show through. His hair had grayed to a yellowish white on either side of the careful, central parting.

"Good evening, Mr. Carter. I hope this is not too inconvenient for you." His English, like the woman's, was nearly perfect.

Carter shook the frail hand. "Well, it is slightly unorthodox."

The man chuckled. "Since you obviously do not recognize me, permit me to introduce myself. I am Pak San Roo."

Carter just stared, bringing a wider smile to the old man's face.

"Of course, Pak San Roo would mean nothing to you. I am also known as the most notorious criminal in Asia, Mr. Carter, under the name Dr. Kwon."

# FIVE

"A shock, I suppose," the old man said, coming around the desk to Carter. "I assume from the startled look on your face, Mr. Carter, that you know something of Dr. Kwon?"

"Oh, yes," the Killmaster replied. "I know the Chinese and the North Koreans wanted him hanged. The South Koreans wanted him at least in jail, and the government of the United States wanted to squeeze him to retrieve even a third of what he stole."

"Quite true, quite true."

"And to the best of my knowledge, Dr. Kwon died fifteen years ago."

This brought a wry smile to the leathery old face. "For all intents and purposes, Dr. Kwon did die. I myself arranged it. But I am afraid that someone has resurrected him." Abruptly, he returned to Kim Li. "My dear, will you tell Koo we will dine on the half hour?"

"Of course."

She slipped from the room and the old man turned back to Carter.

"In time, I will tell you about the making of Dr. Kwon

and his nefarious activities. But first I would like to tell you about Pak San Roo. This way, please."

Carter was led into the subcellar of the big house. It was a highly modern office and communications complex. Telexes clattered, green computer screens blinked, and there was a low hum of radio chatter to and from ships all over the world via satellite.

"Here, Mr. Carter, is the center of my little empire. I say 'little' loosely and use the word 'empire' because that is what it has become in the last fifteen years."

Carter saw stock reports coming in from every exchange in the world. On the computer screens he saw vast sums of money changing hands every second. Even though the hour was late, there were a dozen people working at a furious pace.

"From here I control two shipping lines with several dozen ships at sea at all times. I have a steel foundry in Japan, a plastics factory in Ohio, and a munitions factory in Belgium. There are also a few dozen other assorted companies which I won't bore you with now."

Carter nodded. "I'm convinced."

Pak's face settled into a mask of studied concentration. "Around the world, I would estimate I have twenty thousand employees. And, Mr. Carter, not all of those people are employed solely as money makers. This way, please."

He led Carter to a small elevator that took them silently to the third floor. There, they went down a wide corridor, through an arch, and they were in a large, very modern dining room. The walls were of fine wood paneling and the furnishings could have been sitting in a modern California home.

"Please, sit down," Pak said, dropping into a large chair by an ornate brick fireplace. Kim Li glided into the room. "What will you drink?"

"Scotch," Carter replied.

She nodded.

"Two double scotches," Pak said, "and, of course, sherry for me." He turned to Carter with a silent nod. "My stomach, you see."

Carter was edgy as the woman poured and brought the drinks. He wanted to get to the meat of all this and find out just where this old thief stood, friend or foe. But he forced patience on himself.

"I mentioned that I make a great deal of money. I also spend a great deal. I have built two universities, endowed a half-dozen hospitals. Two of the largest childrens' homes in the world, one right here in Hong Kong, are run with profits from my companies."

"As a conscience balm for old sins?" Carter murmured.

Again the little chuckling laugh. "Quite right, of course. As Dr. Kwon, I was quite an evil person. I consider that was in my youth. Now, in my old age, I think I am quite a good person." Pak raised his glass. "Cheers."

"Cheers," Carter said, and looked at the scotch. "Is this poisoned?"

"Perhaps," Pak laughed. "Kim would be quite capable of it. You Americans, so morbid."

Koo, the butler, came in with a large serving tray.

"Ah, our meal. Let us dine, and I will tell you the story of Dr. Kwon!"


Pak San Roo was born in the mountains of North Korea near Kapsan. His father was a bandit who fought the Japanese, the Russians, and the Chinese all his life.

The young Pak grew up during the Japanese occupation of his country. Both his father and his mother instilled in him a fierce pride in his country and a deep hatred of its many invaders.

By the time World War II broke out, Pak's parents had been killed and he had taken over leadership of the mountain-dwelling bandit army. Throughout the war, young Pak became a spear in the side of the Japanese as they operated out of Korea to invade China.

At the end of the war and Japanese occupation, Pak laid down his arms. But with the partitioning of his country he found that he was once again ruled by a foreign power. Penniless, he fled south to Seoul. But he found only a variation of what he had fled in the north. The government of Syngman Rhee was as corrupt in the south as the Communist government was tyrannical in the north.

Pak San Roo disappeared and Dr. Kwon was born. In the years right after the war, the black market, thievery, prostitution—just about any crime that would make money—flourished in the corrupt government.

Dr. Kwon eventually controlled most of it.

Then the north invaded the south in 1950, and for Dr. Kwon the real boom years began. The Korean won was worth nothing, but U.S. military scrip would buy anything.

On every GI payday, prostitutes seemed to appear out of thin air. They were like ants in the banks of the rivers where the soldiers washed their trucks and Jeeps. They sneaked into the camps at night to share warm nylon-lined sleeping bags with lonely GIs, built villages of cardboard and discarded beer cans along the dusty roads that angled like crooked wagon-wheel spokes from the front. They seemed to be omnipresent.

Toward the middle of the month, when the GIs had spent their money, they would start to disappear. But by that time thousands of dollars in MPCs, presumably for the use of authorized military personnel only, would have been spent at from one dollar to three dollars per roll in the grass. The money went from the girls to an elusive black market organization managed by a mysterious person called Dr. Kwon. Kwon's people, it was said, spirited the monthly fortune in illegal money south into Seoul, the black market center of Yongdungpo and Pusan.

Winding from the isolated town of Yanggu in the tall mountains north of the 38th Parallel, along the Pukhan-Gang River that runs south to the Han River and Seoul, there was a footpath so ancient that the Koreans say it was used by the bloodthirsty hordes of Mongol invaders who overran Korea in the thirteenth century. Before the Japanese built Korea's first roads, this path was the main trade route from north to south. And along this path was said to travel the elusive Dr. Kwon and his couriers with a monthly fortune in MPCs. Yet no one had ever caught Kwon or a nickel of his black-market money.

The military police had tried, so had American and Korean intelligence patrols of the American 45th Division. Dr. Kwon, it seemed, always got through. And the serial number of a marked ten-dollar bill circulated by U.S. intelligence on the first of the month, and spent by a woman-starved GI for a lay in the brown grass of a hillside at Yanggu, would often be traced to Seoul or hundreds of miles south at Pusan only a few days later.

Crime in Korea had always been well organized. It came to the point where Kwon's people had infiltrated everywhere: the police, the government, America's own intelligence, and even the military. His spies were everywhere. When Kwon was after someone, there was no place in Korea to go, no place to hide.

Inchon became a port of call for Dr. Kwon's people to hijack supplies. They had no equal anywhere in the world. Their antics made fools of American intelligence.

And in each year of operation, Dr. Kwon invested more

and more of his ill-gotten gains abroad through Hong Kong banks.

In the early seventies, there was a change in the government. It didn't become a democracy as in the United States, but it did become more responsive to the people. At the same time, the criminal network so carefully put together by Dr. Kwon started to splinter. Their power decreased. Many of the leaders were killed or captured and imprisoned. A few simply disappeared.

Then, in 1974, Dr. Kwon himself was run to ground in Seoul and machine-gunned to death.

Pak San Roo pushed his plate away and motioned to Koo for more wine. As the glasses were filled, Pak continued his tale.

"So you see, Mr. Carter, Dr. Kwon was killed and Pak San Roo was reborn, here in Hong Kong, a respected businessman and philanthropist."

"Do you think," Carter said, leaning across a corner of the table until his face was only inches from the other man's, "that your current philanthropy makes you any less of a son of a bitch?"

The old man didn't even blink. "Not at all. I know it is difficult for your Western mind to grasp, but to the Asian mind, mine and many others, Dr. Kwon and Pak San Roo are two different people. If I had not become Dr. Kwon, Mr. Carter, someone else would have. And, I daresay, he wouldn't have used the money as I am using it now."

Carter sipped his wine. "Such as this reincarnation?"

"Exactly. And that is why we are here." He turned to the woman. "Kim?"

"First of all, Mr. Carter—" she began.

"Let's kill the Mister Carter, okay? Just Nick."

"As you wish, Nick," she replied. "First of all, the man

you were to meet here in Hong Kong, Toby Sukimoto, is dead. He was killed in Detroit before he could even get on the plane."

"The new Dr. Kwon's people?"

"We think so, yes. We have not been able to infiltrate Kwon's organization, but we have been able to learn a great deal about the operation. For quite some time, Ito Sukimoto had been the main link in purchasing all sorts of American government secrets, as well as electronics equipment banned by the United States government to Communist powers."

"He procured all this and sold it to Kwon?" Carter asked.

"Yes. His reasons were twofold. One was pure greed. The other was blackmail."

Pak interrupted. "At one time, Ito Sukimoto was my chief lieutenant in Japan. He was one of those who just disappeared."

"And resurfaced—after your phony death—as a legitimate businessman," Carter offered.

"Exactly," Pak said, nodding. "At the time, I took great pains to erase any trace of those men. Somehow, the person who now calls himself Dr. Kwon has obtained enough information about a few of those men to blackmail them."

Carter refilled his glass with wine in silence, mulling over the confusion of what he had been told.

"What about the son, Toby?"

Kim Li spoke. "Again, Nick, you must understand the Asian mind. Toby Sukimoto hated what his father was doing, but family loyalty would not let him speak out."

Carter turned his attention back to the old man. "Aside from getting rid of this phony Dr. Kwon, what's your stake in this?"

Pak leaned back in his chair and tented his fingers over

his face. "Ah, now we come to the moment of truth. When I first heard that my old organization was being put back together, I didn't worry too much. There will always be crime, and in my own way I could make a few moves that blocked this Kwon from too much power. Even when his wealth started to rise due to selling your American gadgets to Russia, I didn't interfere a great deal. But now there is a new wrinkle . . ."

"The counterfeit money," Carter said.

Pak nodded. "Besides Korean won, counterfeit money is now turning up in great amounts in every major currency in the world. The plates are good, excellent."

"Nick," Kim Li said, "we think the money is all coming from North Korea. And we believe Kwon's ultimate goal is to unify Korea under Communist rule."

"I have little to do with my country now," Pak added, "but there is enough of me left over from my youth to abhor the idea of such a thing coming to pass."

"From my government's standpoint," Carter said, "I know where I stand. But how do I fit with you?"

"As I said before, we have tried to infiltrate Dr. Kwon's organization. It has proven to be impossible. We think you, as a renegade American, could. Once inside, with our help, we think you can learn the identity of this Dr. Kwon."

Carter left it at that. The look that passed between himself and the old man told Carter what would happen to Dr. Kwon once Carter unmasked him.

"I am sorry," Pak said suddenly, his face slightly flushed, "but age is telling on me. It is late. Koo will show you to your rooms. Think hard on your decision, Nick Carter. Together we may be the only solution to this perplexing, and exceedingly dangerous, problem."

For a long time, the old man held Carter's eyes. It was

as though he were examining a steer or a racehorse. There was no smile on his face now, no hostility either, just a shrewd and probing curiosity.

When the butler, Koo, tapped his shoulder, Carter rose and left the room

The bedroom was stunning in its simplicity and its blending of Chinese antiques with modern furniture. The bath was the largest Carter had ever seen. It was done in Italian marble, white with veins of gold. The tub was eight feet long and sunken.

He wasted no time. He ran the tub hot and stripped. At a console bar across from the bed, he built himself a nightcap and sank into the warm water.

Everything Pak San Roo and Kim Li had told him spun like a top in his brain.

There was little doubt that the man had the resources to back Carter up if he went in. But had Pak been truthful about his reasons? Was he still running the underworld in Korea, and simply wanted to use Carter to get rid of an upstart competitor?

All these and a few hundred other questions bombarded Carter's mind as he wrapped a towel around himself and walked into the bedroom.

"This seems to be your night for baths."

She had brushed out her long black hair and tied it back with a simple green ribbon. She had changed into a black negligee. The negligee was shimmery and semitransparent. Also, it was cut low on top and slit high on the skirt so that the material parted. The result was that much of Kim Li's voluptuous body rippled in and out of view as she moved.

The high thrust of the breasts with their scarlet nipples played hide-and-seek with the black lace bodice.

Carter immediately wondered to himself why she had

gone to the trouble of arranging herself so seductively, and came to only one conclusion.

"Are you the 'added incentive' to make me go along with the old man?"

The slight smile disappeared and her features turned to stone. She stepped aside, and on the bed behind her were Carter's tools, the Luger and the stiletto.

"Pak San Roo wanted to make sure you knew you were a guest and not a prisoner. Good night."

Carter caught her by the elbow. "Wait a minute. Maybe I spoke too soon."

"Maybe you did."

"How about a nightcap and some conversation? I'm curious."

"About me?"

"That's right. Where do you fit?"

The little wry smile returned to her lips. "Besides baths, it seems to be a night for life stories."

Carter poured brandy and they settled into two chairs around a small table.

"In answer to your question, any business the size of Mr. Pak's needs an intelligence operation. I run it."

This instantly got Carter's attention. "I'm still curious. How did you get qualified for such a position?"

She bowed her head for several moments, as if she were weighing her answer before speaking. When she looked up, Carter knew he was going to hear it all.

"I told you that my father was Australian. He lived with my mother for two years. When his tour of duty was up, he gave her money and left. She never told him she was pregnant. I was born five months after he left. A year after that, the money ran out and my mother went back to the only business she knew. . ."

"Prostitution," Carter said quietly.

"Yes. When I was ten, she was killed in a fire. As a mixed-race orphan, the state really didn't know what to do with me. I was indentured with several other girls to a farm family in Wonju. I was twelve when the oldest son of the couple raped me. A week later, when he tried again, I slit his throat."

She paused here to register Carter's reaction. When there was none, she continued.

"I ran away to Seoul and took up my mother's profession."

"At thirteen?"

"Yes. The house was owned by Dr. Kwon. I came to his attention because I was already beautiful and spoke English. He took me as a mistress, but I became much more. I have gone to schools in Switzerland and England. For five years I was an operative in the K-CIA. As such, I still served Dr. Kwon, supplying him with information."

Here she finished her drink and set the glass down between them.

"You must be very good," Carter said, "at what you do."

The smile was cold, humorless. "I have always been good at everything I do. If you are wondering if I am capable of providing your backup, you can put it out of your mind. Believe me, I will always be there."

"I believe you," he replied.

"Then you will do it?"

"I'll give you my answer in the morning."

She stood to leave. Carter blocked her path.

"One more thing, Kim Li. If I do agree, and I smell anything along the way, you buy it first."

"Buy it . . . ?"

"I kill you first," he replied.

She met his gaze steadily. "That is entirely understandable. Good night."

Carter slept fitfully, and over an elaborate breakfast the following morning he agreed to go along with Pak San Roo.

The plan was simple but effective. The largest percentage of electronics component parts being shipped to Korea had come from Blue Chip Enterprises in Detroit. With that source gone, Dr. Kwon would be looking for a new source.

Carter would go to Korea as an American thief, one who had stolen electronics gear and sold it to Toby Sukimoto. He had not been paid and was angry. By looking for Sukimoto's girlfriend in Seoul, the only name he had, he hoped to get payment.

Hopefully, this would eventually draw attention to himself, and draw Dr. Kwon's attention as well.

One of Pak's conditions was that Carter simply disappear as Carter from Hong Kong, and reappear in Seoul under the identity provided by Pak.

Carter okayed this in general, but with one stipulation: his immediate superior had to be notified.

Pak didn't like the idea, but when Carter told him it was that way or nothing, he was allowed to use the basement communications gear to contact AXE's founder and director, David Hawk, in Washington.

The go-ahead came back an hour later.

That evening, Carter, armed with papers that AXE itself could not have forged better, was flown secretly into Manila in the Philippines.

The next morning, as retired Major Nicholas Crider of Army Purchasing, he flew commerical on into Seoul.

# SIX

Carter arrived at Kimpo Airport in the early afternoon. He carried only a light bag containing the bare essentials and a single change, but it took him nearly an hour to get through customs. And this with two customs people scrutinizing his luggage and his papers.

He tried to brush away the unusual attention with the excuse that his Nicholas Crider visa was for longer than the fifteen days of a normal tourist.

"You travel light for such a long stay, Mr. Crider."

"Yes. Because of your marvelous tailors and materials, I plan on purchasing an entire new wardrobe here."

"I see. On your passport you are self-employed. What is your employment, Mr. Crider?"

"I am a small manufacturer...micropackaging and conductors."

"Do you plan on doing business in Korea?"

"No, this is strictly vacation."

The questioning went on and on. It could have been normal, because a record of every tourist entry is passed on to the police, but still....

Pak San Roo had said that the new Dr. Kwon had followed his own format from years before of placing his own people in the police and government. Could this extensive interrogation be taking place because Kwon had been tipped that Carter was coming?

At last, "Have a nice stay in our country, Mr. Crider."

"Thank you."

It was unseasonably humid as Carter stepped from the terminal. He felt the wall of it as he waited in line for a cab.

So far, Pak had been crafty in all his instructions. Carter had entered the country unarmed. Getting a gun would be the first step in letting Dr. Kwon know he was around. Kim Li would smuggle Carter's own Luger and stiletto in later.

"What hotel, sir?"

"Seoul Garden," Carter replied, and slid into the cab.

He settled back with a cigarette as the driver fought the ten miles of traffic to the center of the city.

Pak had supplied him with a list of twenty-six names, nineteen women and seven men. According to him, any one of these twenty-six knew enough about the old organization to bring it out of the ashes and re-create it as the new Dr. Kwon had done.

At first, Pak had given Carter only twelve names. The other fourteen were dead. But the Killmaster had insisted upon them all, dead or alive. An intricate organization such as Pak had originally set up could be passed on if records had been kept.

They had both agreed that one of the names on the list was bound to be the record keeper.

Then there was the last piece of information—and warning—from Pak:

"Whoever Kwon is, he stays in the background, in the

shadows. A man by the name of Jacques Bonner runs the everyday operation. Bonner is the gun and the muscle."

Pak didn't have to give Carter a rundown on Jacques Bonner. Carter and every police force and intelligence organization in the Far East knew about the man.

He had been one of the prime movers of raw opium out of the Golden Triangle during the Vietnam War. When that got too hot for him, Bonner had moved into gambling and prostitution in Singapore. Chased out of there, he had gone into smuggling, dope, white slavery, and murder, between Indochina and Hong Kong.

Jacques Bonner had never been arrested or convicted of a crime, but he had a "watch" record with Interpol as long as his arm.

Jacques Bonner had disappeared for a while after a huge shipment of Russian arms had been tagged going to Communist rebels in the Philippines with his mark all over them.

When he surfaced again, it was in Korea, running the show for Dr. Kwon.

"How, with his record," Carter had asked Pak, "does he operate so easily in Korea?"

"A record of suspicion," Pak had replied, "not conviction. Also, I am sorry to say, the proper amount of money applied in the proper places would allow almost anyone alien residency in South Korea."

Carter had smiled. "You should know."

"The Seoul Garden, sir."

Carter filled the driver's hand with won, and entered the deluxe hotel. He didn't even pause at the desk, but the bag he carried was a shoulder variety that could double as a camera bag, so he drew no attention.

Through the lobby, he passed the coffee shop and exited by a side door. The Seoul Garden was in the Mapo district.

About twelve blocks away was the shopping and nightlife section of Seoul, the Itaewon area.

It was about a half hour's leisurely walk, and Carter checked into the Crown, on Yong San-ku.

He ordered a bottle of scotch from the bellman and unpacked as he waited. When it came, he built a drink and moved to the tiny terrace outside his room. Through two drinks, he watched the hordes of people as they scurried beneath his window.

When dusk started to settle, he called down to the desk and told the clerk to have a rental car brought around, any kind as long as it ran, had a full tank of gas, a spare, decent tires on the ground, and enough shock absorbers left so it didn't bottom like a tank climbing a wall when he ran over matchsticks.

He showered and shaved, dressed, went down and signed for the car, tipped the kid who brought it around, went into the restaurant and ate dinner. It was only seven-thirty, but fully dark when he left.

He retrieved the car from the lot across the street and drove for an hour aimlessly. By the time the city was pure neon, he returned to the Itaewon area and a gas station he had already spotted near one of the gates to the U.S. Army base.

The station owner was only too happy to take Carter's won to provide him a parking space for twenty-four hours.

From the station, he walked deep into the nightlife of the Itaewon. Between here and the great south gate of the city—the area called Namdaemun—anything could be bought or sold.

He moved through basement shops and bars where everything was on display, from silk and porcelain souvenirs to a pretty woman.

Eventually he found himself in the maze of alleys

known as the "ghost market," a place that went through cycles of high and low visibility, depending on the current mood of the police.

This particular night it looked as if all the necessary payoffs had been made. Business was brisk. It would take a blind man not to see the illegal goods being passed from hand to hand.

Carter wasn't an old hand in Korea, but he was not a stranger, either. It took him about a half hour to spot his man. He was young and hip. He walked with a swagger, and in a two-block walk he had stopped and talked to several not-so-well-dressed men. He spoke and they listened, respectfully, with their heads down; they nodded at once to everything the natty young man said. The man neither gestured nor raised his voice.

Carter waited until he stopped talking before he attempted to catch the man's eye.

The young man approached him halfway and stopped, waiting for Carter to traverse the remaining half, which he did.

"You wish something?" The young man spoke softly, a little hoarsely. His eyes were black, his skin dark brown. He was several inches shorter than Carter and held himself like a compressed spring.

"A gun," Carter said.

A flicker of a smile crossed the young man's face, and faded. "What kind, and in what condition?"

"A thirty-eight in new or good condition."

"No thirty-eights," came the reply. "How about a nice Beretta nine-millimeter?"

"What else do you have?"

The man spread his hands palms up and expansively. "Some excellent forty-fives, American. Brand-new, some of them, with holsters and clips."

"How much?"

"One thousand dollars. American dollars."

"I think the sun has boiled your brains," Carter said calmly, "or perhaps you have an advanced case of syphilis and your brain is beginning to rot. Three hundred dollars."

The little Korean laughed and raised his knee to slap it. "I think my esteemed friend has shoved his poker into the same woman, because his brain is almost nonexistent. Seven hundred dollars."

They settled on five hundred. Carter gave him half and waited in a bar, where he drank bottled beer on the premise that its contents hadn't been adulterated. It was the kind of bar where you had to take that possibility into consideration.

The young man returned before Carter could finish his first bottle of beer. He carried a canvas shopping bag; heads of lettuce and onion shoots poked above the top. He sat at the table opposite Carter, who slipped the money underneath. For a second, their hands touched. The Korean's was a little sweaty; Carter's was bone dry.

When the man left, the shopping bag sat at Carter's feet. He drank another beer and left. He hadn't been able to examine the gun. If it turned out to be a bad one, he was out five bills. But even in the smoke-filled bar, he'd smelled the oil and new leather.

He had no reason to believe anyone would follow him, but he never relaxed his wariness. No one followed him. But at no time did he assume he wouldn't be tailed. In the privacy of a men's room stall in another bar, he examined his merchandise.

The gun was new and in perfect working order. The firing pin glistened, its sharpness almost jewellike. The holster was of the shoulder type. Carter shrugged off his jacket and put it on. After putting the jacket on again, he was satisfied that the weapon made no bulge. With the gun loaded and concealed, he put the two extra clips in separate pockets, and left the bar.

He headed toward the Han River and the area of bars, brothels, and other clip joints that American GIs had once called the "Hellhole."

Somewhere in that area, he was going to find Toby Sukimoto's old girlfriend.

While Nick Carter headed for the Hellhole in Seoul, K-CIA subchief Lee San Kyo slid onto a stool at one of the roulette tables at the Empire Casino five hours by road to the south, in Pusan.

Narrowing his eyes against the smoke curling upward from the brown cigarette in the corner of his lips, he placed a half-million-won chip on double-0.

As the wheel revolved and caught the glitter from the overhead lights, Kyo tried to display some interest in the outcome. It was difficult. The array of beautiful foreign tourists drew his eyes to the rest of the room. Also, he knew that he would win.

His knowledge did not derive from a gambler's belief or hunch. Lee San Kyo was no gambler. His knowledge was born of fact.

On the first Friday of every month, Kyo had walked into the Empire Casino and placed a won chip worth about $625 on double-0. The wheel would spin and Kyo would move to the bar with the approximate equivalent in won of $13,000.

The first Friday of every month was very profitable for Kyo. But now his little windfall was ending and he was depressed.

That afternoon, the voice on the phone had told him that

there would be an interruption in the shipments. The voice didn't say for how long.

If it was for too long, say more than three months, it could be disastrous for Kyo. He had invested heavily in the Japanese stock market, buying short. There were the un-limited expenses of his mistress, and the house he was building on Cheju Island.

He had the income from his other illegal activities, of course, but without the money from the regular delivery to Seoul, he would soon go under.

The foreign tourists standing around the table craned their necks and gasped, their own greed whetted by Kyo's enormous win.

With a nonchalance that was almost awe-inspiring, he gathered his chips and moved toward the cage to have them cashed. The features of his handsome face were immobile and his slender, athletic body seemed to float beneath the gray silk suit covering it.

After pocketing the money, he drifted to the bar. With-out a word, the bartender placed a large snifter of Rémy Martin brandy in front of him. He never drank the milky *soju* or the spicy *anju*, or even Korean beer. Like so many other facets of Kyo's life, his tastes in drink were decidedly Western, and expensive.

Kyo looked elegant, standing at the bar in his hand-tai-lored suit from Seoul's version of London's Savile Row. His thick black hair glistened under the casino's lights, and when women looked at him, he smiled into their eyes to show his even white teeth. He would have liked to take that pretty blond Englishwoman home with him. It was clear she wanted to be taken home. Clear, too, that she'd already been told, "That's Lee San Kyo, the chief inspector in the K-CIA criminal division in Pusan. An important man."

But not tonight, my juicy yellow-haired one, Kyo told himself without taking his eyes off her body and hungry blue eyes. You see, dear lady, tonight Lee San Kyo ensures the ease of his retirement.

A flash of white at the end of the bar drew his eye. He looked, and found himself staring into the blue orbs of ice that only their owner, Jacques Bonner, would call eyes. The chiseled jaw and high cheekbones nodded and the white suit moved away through the crowd.

The shipment, in its waterproof pouch, was ready.

Kyo shivered and he drank the rest of his Rémy Martin and paid. Jacques Bonner always had that effect on him.

He glanced at the Rolex on his wrist. In five hours he would be through Seoul. Another forty-five minutes north and he would be at the rendezvous . . . usually.

But not tonight.

He said good night to those who knew him, and stepped outside. He could not see the man who called himself Ho Shan, but he knew he was out there, waiting.

That was the worst of it, and, to Kyo, the most dangerous. He had told Bonner this.

"No, there is hardly any chance at all that my car, an official car, would ever be stopped, even that close to the DMZ. But what if it were? How could I explain an armed man who is not an agent in the car with me?"

"Ho Shan will accompany you on each trip."

Kyo had protested again vehemently, and Bonner had chilled his soul with those blue eyes.

"Ho Shan goes with you. Consider it for your own safety, Kyo, so you never get curious enough to look inside those waterproof packages and see what you are carrying."

The harbor lights winked good-naturedly at Kyo as he gulped the sea air. He put a cigarette between his lips and lit it. He lit the lighter a second time, let it flicker in the breeze for ten seconds, and snapped the cover shut. He knew that Ho had seen the signal, knew at this moment the man was getting into the passenger side of Kyo's Cressida and had a pistol pointed at the window. Ho was an untrusting man.

Kyo opened the driver's door and slid behind the wheel. Not until he'd started the engine and put the big car into motion did either man speak. Ho slid the pistol into a shoulder holster. His almost black, liquid eyes searched Kyo's face for a moment, then flicked into neutral.

Ho Shan was stocky, almost squat. Under a very thin, smooth layer of fat lay coiled an enormous wellspring of muscle. He presented a stark contrast beside the slender, elegantly catlike Kyo.

"Something wrong?" he said, noticing Kyo's eyes flicker toward him as they wound through the streets toward the new Seoul highway.

"No, I was remembering that this is the last time . . . for a while."

Suddenly Ho smiled, showing yellow teeth, and cackled. "Yes, the last time, for a while, we have to visit and smell the shit, man."

As Kyo hit the highway and picked up speed, he thought of the Englishwoman in the casino who had begged him with her eyes and body to be taken.

She had been attractive. But not as attractive as the profit from this night would be.

No woman was that attractive.

But even as Kyo thought this, he remembered Bonner's eyes, and shivered again.

# SEVEN

The Hellhole hadn't changed too much since the last time Carter had seen it. Some of the broken neons had been repaired. So had a few windows. The smell was the same, and dirt still poked up through the cracks in the sidewalks.

The names, too, hadn't changed very much: Cherry Bar, Club Far East, New York Bar, Chicago Bar, and on and on.

By eleven o'clock, he had hit eight or nine of them, and he was getting bloated from the Crown beer and sushi snacks.

He rounded the corner of yet another narrow alley that sported another vast array of winking signs. He chose one called Big Mamma's, and pushed through the door.

Cigarette smoke, stale beer, and the drifting scents of a dozen perfumes assaulted his nostrils. Music, if it could be called that, blared from a half-dozen speakers around the room.

A girl came gliding from neon shadows, sashaying in a tight red gown that plunged low between the cones of her breasts. Midnight hair cascaded richly over ivory shoulders; ripe lips smiled for him. She had almond eyes that clung to his, and she was a woman, her smell touched with sandalwood and spices.

"Hello," she said, and put a pale, weightless hand against his arm. "You like table or bar?"

"A table," Carter said.

As she led him to a booth, he searched the shadowed corners of the bar. At one table a girl dealt herself a hand of solitaire. Three more at another table looked bored. A young Korean couple occupied a booth, and two American GIs jawed with a girl at the bar.

It was a slow night at Big Mamma's.

Carter ordered the usual beer and a side dish of snacks.

"You like to buy Suzy a drink?"

Carter smiled. "Sure."

She scooted away, and a lacquered face belonging to three hundred pounds of woman lumbered through a curtain behind the bar.

As the woman got the drinks, a wiry little man darted through the door and went right to the bar. He leaned halfway over it and carried on a hurried and whispered conversation with Lacquer Face.

Both of them shot a glance Carter's way, and the little man rushed out.

*Well, well*, Carter thought, *maybe I am ruffling a few feathers*.

Suzy came back with a tray, beer, sushi, and a glass containing a splash of wine over crushed ice. She set the drinks around and moved into the booth until her thigh was pressed hotly against Carter's.

"What's your name?"

"Nick."

"You're not GI?"

"No, businessman."

"Then you never been to Big Mamma's before. We have private hostess rooms in back."

"Maybe later," Carter said with a smile. "I've been here before, but I don't remember you. Have you worked here long?"

She concentrated with a sip of her diluted wine. "Almost four years."

"Then you probably remember a girl I met in here a long time ago. Her name was Tomiko...Tomiko Mochiko."

She chewed on her lip for a moment, and then shook her head. "No, I don't remember her ever working here."

Suddenly the light was gone, obscured by the bulk of Big Mamma at Carter's elbow. "No Tomiko here. You got wrong place."

Carter stared into the face that showed him nothing. "You sure?"

The behemoth shrugged. "Maybe, maybe not. All time, girls go, girls come. You take this girl Suzy. She give you good time."

The girl's eyes shuttered as she stared into the melting remains of her drink.

"I have to find the other girl," Carter said.

"You"—Suzy's voice faltered, but she caught the owner looking at her and went on—"you do not like me? I-I be good to you, nice time."

Carter shoved her the change from the bill. "Hang on to this and have a few drinks. I may be back."

"Come back, please."

He touched her hand and left. There were other bars crowding the street; Tomiko could be in any of them.

But where?

Tomiko Mochiko was a Japanese name. She was a Japanese woman working in Korea. Someone had to remember her.

The crowds on the street were getting heavier. Seoul was a nighttime city with late-night people.

He pushed on, and had no luck in the Club Opal or the Fat Cat Club. Six more, working himself up the other side of the street, were the same.

Each of them was like a clone of the next or the last—stools, booths along one wall, toilets in back, and beyond them, the courtyard and rooms. All were crowded. All were noisy and smoky and drunken. Some women were cheerful and some were sullen, but all were pretty.

None of them was named Tomiko Mochiko.

At one in the morning Carter found himself back in front of Big Mamma's. He remembered the look that had passed between the girl, Suzy, and the fat woman.

He also remembered the little ferretlike man who had run in with the whispered conversation.

Carter was just sliding onto a barstool, when he realized that, unlike the other bars in the area, Big Mamma's was quiet. There wasn't a customer in the place.

He didn't see the girl, Suzy, but the rest of the girls were huddled in one of the booths. None of them looked at him and one of them came up to the bar to cadge a watered-down drink.

He was in now and he was going to stay, even when a muscular young man in a dark suit came through the curtain instead of Lacquer Face.

"You like a beer?"

"Yeah."

He opened a bottle, grabbed a glass, and poured. "On the house."

"Thanks." Carter saluted and sipped.

"Big Mamma here say you look for certain girl."

"That's right. Tomiko Mochiko."

"Japanese name."

"That's right," Carter said.

The young man laughed. It was a dead sound in the middle of the scale without going up or down. "Why you want Japanese girl? We got lots of beautiful Korean girls."

"This girl has a friend, a boyfriend. I can't find the boyfriend, so I thought I'd look her up and maybe she could put me on to him."

"You must want to find this boyfriend bad."

"I do."

"Why?"

Carter grinned. "Let's just say he owes me some money . . . lots of money."

"What's this boyfriend's name? I mean, I might be able to help you after all."

Carter spread the grin. "None of your business."

"I think you maybe better tell me."

Carter spread the grin from ear to ear and leaned close. "Fuck you. You understand that, don't you? Fuck you."

They converged out of everywhere . . . a booth, from behind the curtain, and out of the hall leading to the toilets. Carter could scarcely tell one from the other: high cheekbones, narrow, hooded eyes, brush-cut black hair, and dark suits.

The first man rammed in with head down. Carter took a pair of steps to one side and kicked him in the face. He spun off the kick and cartwheeled into the bar.

The second man reached in low and snakelike, the slim blade in his fist angled up. Carter rolled his shoulders to the right, then swayed left and picked up the incoming wrist as the knifer followed the feint.

Turning, bringing the arm down across his hip, Carter grunted with sudden effort as he brought the man around

hard and fast to run him into the wall. The man grunted
back, staggered back as Carter let go of the wrist. Carter
hit him twice . . . short, vicious blows that damn near tore
off his head.

The one at the bar was on his knees, so Carter kicked
him again. The third man backed up a step, another, and
snatched at the empty wine bottle on a table. Carter's left
hand scooped up a barstool and brought it whistling around
as the man skipped desperately away, waving the bottle.

He broke for the window as Carter flung the stool. The
man went down in a tangle of legs and a flailing of arms.
The bottle crashed away.

Too late, Carter saw the one he had been talking to at
the bar coming over. He whirled, digging the .45 from
under his jacket, but the man was a master. One foot
kicked the gun from Carter's hand. The other caught him
square in the face.

Carter went down with all four of them on him.

It was still a pretty good brawl, but the odds were
against him now. Feet and fists were everywhere, and all of
them were landing on his head and body.

Then there was a slight lull, and through a bloody haze
he saw the face of the man from behind the bar right over
his.

"Leave Korea. Forget the money this man, Sukimoto,
owes you. It is lost. And forget Tomiko Mochiko. I say
again, leave Korea."

Then the kicking started again. Just before Carter passed
out, he folded into a fetal position and smiled to himself.

He hadn't mentioned Sukimoto's name. The hotshot
with the fast feet did.

The ball was starting to roll.

•   •   •

Kyo was sweating heavily as he slowed the car for the warning checkpoint at Munson. A few miles on to the north was Panmunjom and the Demilitarized Zone. To the west was the inlet that led out to Kanghwa Bay.

The soldiers recognized the car and license plate. Then they recognized the man driving. As always, Kyo pulled into the area by the observation post and got out.

Fifteen minutes elapsed, during which Kyo and the officer in charge drank tea, bemoaned the constant threat of aggression from the North, children, women, and how damned hard life could be.

"Any trouble?" the thick-bodied gunman asked when Kyo returned to the car.

"I don't think so," Kyo replied, pasting a worried look on his face.

"What do you mean?"

Kyo shrugged. "Probably nothing, but they have reports of some strange activity in the area tonight."

About three miles up the main road, Kyo wheeled the car to the left into a tiny dirt road almost hidden by trees and bushes. About four miles ahead was the mouth of the inlet where the *Honey Pot* would be waiting.

Kyo hoped that his pistol-carrying passenger wouldn't notice his tension. After all, this monthly trip north and back was almost wholly without risk. Who would dare search or question a top K-CIA agent in the pursuit of his duty? Besides, Kyo told himself, every detail had been worked out. It was stupid to worry, stupid to risk displaying any nervousness.

But still he could feel the sweat soaking the back of his shirt.

There would be at least three of them, well armed.

*Stop worrying*, Kyo told himself, *it will go as planned*.

He lit another cigarette from the stubby butt of the one he had smoked.

Beside Kyo, Ho Shan found himself wondering why the K-CIA man was smoking so much tonight. The man was a smoker, yes, but usually not this heavy. It was a bad habit, smoking. Bad for the lungs, bad for a man like Ho, who had to run fast or climb steep hills or swim rivers on missions of killing for Dr. Kwon.

The beauty of the plan, Kyo thought as he drove, would be his own surprise. He had no inkling where it would happen. They had not told him, and he had not wanted to know.

Now every bend in the road, every new clump of heavy trees became a possible spot.

This would be a good spot, Kyo thought.

But that spot was passed.

They were less than a mile from the water. It would have to be soon, very soon.

Even with his anticipation and prior knowledge, it seemed to surprise Kyo more than Ho when it actually happened. Ho's pistol was already aimed at the windshield. The headlights picked out the barbed wire stretching waist-level across the road. Then they spotted them: five men. Kyo saw two shotguns. Another man carried an automatic weapon. The barrels waved at them like frantically undulating trees against a gale wind. Shots cracked through the darkness. Kyo felt the car bumping and swerving on flat tires. A stray bullet shattered the rear window on his side.

He stopped the car.

Three men held submachine guns on them while two searched the car. One of them yanked the keys from the ignition and moved to the trunk while another leveled a double-barreled shotgun at Ho's head.

All quite clever, Kyo thought. They'd pretended uncertainty as to the package's location by searching the inside of the car first. They'd even gone so far as to shoot out the tires and a window. It would be obvious to Ho that Kyo had no idea what was going on. The K-CIA man had been genuinely surprised.

But Ho now knew why the man had smoked so many cigarettes during the evening. The bastards had missed one important move: they'd neglected to disarm Kyo. Minor . . . but revealing. And stupid, quite stupid. Now he saw them put the package into the back seat of a waiting pickup truck.

"Move over there!" one of the gunmen ordered Ho.

Ho moved in the direction indicated. If they had any sense at all, they'd shoot him and bury him. In six months, someone might find his bones. He thought of his wife. Dr. Kwon would provide for her. She would have shelter; she would not go hungry. Knowing that, and finding comfort in the knowledge, Ho was completely ready to die. In this business, only an idiot dreamed of immortality and old age.

Yes, it was a good setup. Admirable. One with less experience than he had would find it all most convincing, Ho thought as he watched one of the gunmen toss Kyo into the back of the truck.

Now they were ready to kill. Now he would die, surely. Tomorrow the sun would rise and burn away this humid air and he would be bones.

For a moment, one of the shotgun-wielding men smiled into Ho's face. Then, in a blurred motion, he swung the weapon like a baseball bat, two-handed, and smashed Ho across the forehead. He fell to the ground.

He heard the sounds of his ears pounding, his blood rushing, felt bile and vomit rise in his guts from the pain.

Then, nothing.

He never heard Kyo cry out, "Damn, you fool, do not kill him! He must live to tell them what happened!"

It was nearly an hour before Ho clawed his way back to consciousness. The light mist that had fogged the windshield earlier had now turned to rain. This helped to wash the blood from his eyes and the cobwebs of dizziness from his brain.

It was painful. It took him several more minutes to recall what had happened and where he was, several more minutes to focus his mind and move himself.

Walking became less painful after a while. The stench from the barge, the *Honey Pot*, led him like a beacon. The old smuggler, Twan Khai, would have a motorbike on board. Ho would take it and find a telephone.

There would be no delivery to North Korea tonight.

The blood had coagulated into a scabby cover on his head. It throbbed like a bark from all the hounds of hell.

But Ho kept walking.

He walked upright without staggering because he had felt pain worse than this many times in his life.

And no man who had ever caused him pain had ever remained alive to boast of it.

Tomiko Mochiko stood before Jacques Bonner, trying to keep the fear from her eyes. Beneath the kimono, her naked body was trembling.

This was the second time she had been summoned. Her body still bore the bruises from the first encounter.

Bonner's eyes lewdly stripped the garment from her as he moved like a cat around her. He was nude, and she became fascinated by the coils of muscle that rippled beneath his skin.

He had started drinking at the casino. He had not been drunk the first time he had ordered her to his rooms, and he had been a sadistic beast. With drink, what would he be like tonight?

"Are you afraid?" he asked.

"Yes."

"Good. That will make it all more exciting. Don't you agree?"

Tomiko said nothing, and trembled harder as his hand moved over her body.

"Being one of my women is a small price to pay for the security you have now, isn't it, Tomiko?"

"Yes," she replied, and swallowed.

"Your success with Sukimoto was excellent. We knew every move the fool was going to make before he made it. I could see that in you long ago, when you were just a bar girl. The blood of a seductress flows in your veins and shows in your eyes." His voice became a low whisper at her ear. "Seduce me, Tomiko-san."

The woman was frozen, immobile. The blow, when it came, whirled her across the room.

Then he was at her, his teeth grinding against hers in an obscene kiss as he dragged her back to her feet.

"Where is your passion, woman?" he hissed. "Show me the passion I pay you for!"

When she still remained silent, Bonner curled his fingers brutally into the thick richness of her hair. Suddenly he flung her across the room. She landed on the bed with one ivory-skinned leg outstretched, her mouth and eyes wide.

He peeled her out of the ripped garment as if he were pulling the skin from a banana, exposing her flesh like the soft meat of the fruit. With a cry of frustration and anger, Tomiko tried to crawl away from him.

Bonner caught her ankle and snatched her roughly back toward him. Whirling, she came over onto her back and tried to use her other foot on him. He slapped the leg aside and went swiftly between her knees. She daggered fingernails at his eyes. He pinned both her wrists in one hand while his other roamed freely over her naked body, clutching and cupping and making her know she could not resist, that she could do nothing he did not want her to.

Tomiko whined like a trapped animal when his mouth went to the base of her throat, when his heavy body put its weight on top of her. She went rigid, stiff in hatred and motionless with the shock of him, the driving, not-to-be-denied power of him.

She didn't scream. He didn't give a damn if she did.

Tomiko fought him silently, not with supplication, but with the fury of her body, with the raging clasp of her thighs and the hammering of her breasts. She clung to him, tried to strangle him with her silken flesh, to drown him in the tidal surgings of her hips. She fought, arching and clamping and devouring, locked to him and with him in a stormy madness that shook him, that turned the world red-black, red-black, until at last he tore himself apart on a glittering peak and fell in twisting, floating pieces back down the hillside.

As he spasmed, he laughed aloud, adding to the insult of the rape.

The phone was ringing insistently as he rolled off her body.

"Nae?"

"This is Ho Shan. We have been betrayed."

Bonner listened, the hot blood of anger filling his body as the blood of lust had filled it moments before.

"The man is a fool!"

"He is that," Ho replied. "Greed has expanded his balls and turned his brain to mush."

"How badly are you hurt?"

"I can travel."

"Good. Get back here. We will pinch Lee San Kyo for our goods, and if they are not returned, our friend in the K-CIA will provide the squid of the ocean with nourishment."

"As you wish," Ho replied. *"Anyong-ee."*

Jacques Bonner dropped the instrument back on its cradle and turned to the cringing woman on the bed.

"Now, my lovely one, where were we?"

# EIGHT

Carter groaned aloud as the doctor finished binding the tape and thick bandage around his chest. He also kept his red, swollen eye averted from the harsh glare of the sun through the window.

He had awakened sometime just before dawn in an alley near the river, far from the bar. Luckily, his head had been resting on a curb or he might have drowned in the puddles caused by the sudden heavy rain.

After making sure he was going to live, he got a cruising taxi and made it back to the hotel. The night staff barely noticed his condition. They were used to crazy Americans.

In the room, he hadn't even taken off his clothes, just flopped across the bed, wet, dirty, and bloody.

The next morning was a different story. He knew he needed to have a doctor at least look at him. He ordered one along with breakfast.

"You shouldn't drink so much, Mr. Crider."

"Yeah, I know. I'm always falling downstairs like this."

The doctor's smile said it all: *Bullshit*.

"What's the verdict?" Carter asked, mashing out a freshly lit cigarette because it hurt to breathe.

"Besides bruises, which will heal quickly, you have one cracked rib and I took nine stitches in your head. You really should come to my office. You might have a concussion."

"I'll take my chances. Thanks, Doc."

He dropped a handful of big won bills on the table, and sat down to his breakfast.

The doctor shrugged, poked through the bills until he had enough for his fee, and left.

Carter managed half the breakfast before pushing away from the table and returning to the bed.

It was midafternoon when the telephone rang. The switchboard operator told him that his ticket for that evening's performance of Chopin at the National Classical Music Institute was reserved.

It was the word from Kim Li that she was in and had her ducks set up in a row to operate.

He climbed into his last set of clothes, packed his bag, and hit the lobby. After making a production out of checking out, he grabbed a cab and told the driver, "Kimpo Airport."

Just outside the city, Carter looked out the rear window for the first time, and saw a black Toyota maneuvering with every move the taxi driver made.

Carter wasn't surprised. They'd told him to get out of Korea, and they were tailing him to make sure he followed orders.

At the airport Carter told his driver to pull out of the line and park. He paid him three times what the meter read.

"Will that hire you for a few hours?"

"Oh, yes, sir. But you catch plane?"

"Not for another three hours," Carter said. "I want a last

little fling before I leave Korea. You understand?"

"Ah, you like spend time with girl?"

"You got it," Carter replied. "Is there a real first-class place near the airport?"

"Ah, yes, very close, Lompii district. Is called House of All Countries. Number One girl from France, Germany, Africa, all over. Even catch fine blond American girl."

"How sweet it is," Carter mumbled. "I'll be right back."

Inside the terminal, he bought a ticket for a KAL flight to Tokyo that left at seven that evening, and checked his bag. From the counter he moved to the foreign exchange counter and changed the two thousand in traveler's checks Pak had given him into won.

Stuffing the money into his inside jacket pocket, he returned to the cab. As they left the airport, the Toyota and its three occupants were right on Carter's tail.

The House of All Countries was a pagodalike structure taking up half a block on a busy street in the Lompii district.

Carter shoved a few thousand more won into the driver's hand. "You relax, eat, drink, whatever. Just wait and take me back to the airport."

The driver shrugged and counted the money as Carter climbed a double set of stone steps. One side of a double door led him into a dim, cool foyer. Here he paused and peered back toward the street through one of the narrow panes of colored glass.

He watched the taxi driver amble across the street and enter a tearoom. Then he smiled as one of the dark suits from the Toyota went in right after him.

"Hello, won't you enter the House of All Countries?"

She was short, petite, and wore the traditional flowing Korean dress gathered tightly beneath her small breasts. She had to be about fifty, but there wasn't a wrinkle in her face. She smiled and Carter was almost blinded from the glare of gold in her mouth.

"I am Madame Cho. Please come in."

"Why, I'll sure as hell do that, little lady. Ah just come from ol' Kimpo Airport. Got to catch me a flight home, but I got me a few hours, an' I thought ah'd get me a little last fling of poontang 'fore ah go!"

All this as she led him through the halls and into a room warm with incense, soft colors, and hanging Chinese tapestries. Carter saw that the house was a fine old building that smelled of class and the gentility of another day.

The woman guided him to a sea of cushions and clapped her hands. Two young girls breezed in with trays as muted music filled the air from hidden speakers. In seconds tea was served and the girls had disappeared.

"Hot damn, now this is what ah'd call a class cathouse!"

The woman's lips pinched at the sides but her face remained stoic. "Let me inquire, sir, as to your tastes?"

"Missus Cho, ma'am, my tastes is women. Ah'm from the South, ma'am, where most of what we got fer amusement is the three R's . . . racin', rasslin', and religion. So while ah'm here in the Orient away from the little woman, ah'm wantin' some real whoopee! Ya get mah drift?"

He was breaking her façade. There was a pained look coming into her features. Carter would lay ten to one that once he was in the room with a girl, Madame Cho wouldn't bother her. She wouldn't want to have to talk to him again.

She clapped her hands and the passing parade began.

"This is Tora, from Bombay."

The first girl was a soft-eyed Indian beauty in a sari. She moved as if there were nothing but air under her feet, and her smile was a whisper of great promise. Carter let out a whoop when she opened her sari and he saw that beneath it she was stark naked.

"My, oh, my, my!"

"Would you like Tora, sir?"

"Hell, ma'am, ah don't know. Ah'm like a hog wallerin' at the trough. Let's see 'em all!"

"Nina is a White Russian born in Hong Kong."

Nina wore transparent gauze that hugged here and billowed there. She smiled, whirled to expose all of her perfect body, and, when Carter showed no interest, drifted on out of the room.

Next came Paola, fresh from the hot sands of Algeria.

Paola's raven hair clustered in tight ringlets on her slim, dark neck. She wore a simple white gown that accented her glossy ebony skin. It was wrapped tightly to outline each curve, and although she was willowy, she had curves.

They became a passing blur . . . Gerta from Germany, blond and tall, Old World and bouncy in a frankly feminine nightie. Norelle next, buxom with pale skin. Mai Ling with a tiny body moving in soft silk.

"This girl," the madam said, "will burn in your bed like a fire. She is Mogabe, from darkest Africa."

Mogabe was a lot of woman, over six feet, and all of it draped in shimmering scarlet cloth that left nothing to the imagination. Her velvety black skin glowed with dark fires, and Carter could almost hear jungle drums and smell palm oil when she swung past, her erect, muscled body regally savage.

At the door she turned her head over her shoulder and winked. Her jaw also started going ninety miles an hour on a wad of bubble gum.

"Next, sir . . ." the madam said.

"Don't need no next," Carter said. "I want that one!"

"Ah, Mogabe very expensive . . . very talented."

"I'll bet. How much?"

"Three hundred American dollar."

Carter peeled off the bills and dropped them in her lap. "Hot damn, ma'am, don't ring the bell for three hours!"

He was out of the room and up the stairs as he saw the tall black girl dart into a room. He crashed in behind her and slid the door closed.

She was already half out of the scarlet wraparound and draped across the bed. "Oog-ah-loo."

Carter dropped his own act. "Oog-ah-loo, hell, honey, where are you from?"

"Brooklyn."

"I thought so," he growled, opening the inner doors and checking the gardens and a tall stone wall beyond.

"You ain't exactly a dumb cracker either, honey," she chuckled. "What's your scam?"

"I need a back way out of here and a three-hour head start." He pulled the wad of Korean money out of his pocket. "How much?"

She eyed the wad, Carter, and licked her lips. "A one way ticket back to the U.S. of A."

"What's your real name?"

"Gloria."

"You drive a hard bargain, Gloria."

"You may be my last chance out of this rathole."

"What's the story?" he asked. "Not that I care."

She shrugged. "You probably heard it before. Strip joint in Japan. It didn't last. Better offer over here, except the job turned out to be in this classy dump. I was broke, what can I say."

"You're right, but if you can get me out of here, you've got a deal."

She moved to stand behind him at the window and pointed across the garden. "There's a bath house out there individual rooms. Hall between the rooms ends in a door in the wall. It's the way the servants come and go."

"Swell. How do we get from here to there?"

"No sweat," she said, and turned into a whirlwind.

Twenty minutes later she was dressed with a large Japanese-style kimono thrown on over her clothes. Carter was the same with his trousers rolled up. Their shoes were rolled in two towels.

"Where does that alley back there go?" he asked.

"Into another alley, and another, and another. Comes out about a mile from here on a main drag by the expressway. We can get a taxi there."

"Lead on!" Carter said.

She stopped him at the terrace door with a hand on his elbow. "I can trust you, can't I, fellow traveler?"

Carter gave her what was left of the won he'd gotten at the airport, as well as the KAL ticket he'd bought. "You can put your name on that and have it reissued at the airport. In fact, you can make that flight."

She brushed her lips across his cheek. "If ya ever get to Brooklyn, sport, it's Gloria Stratford. I'm in the book."

The way she looked now, Carter almost wished he could waste a little of the three hours.


Carter directed the new taxi driver back to the gas station in Seoul. From there, Gloria took the cab to Kimpo Airport.

The Killmaster retrieved the rental car and left the city on the Yangdong Expressway toward Kangnung in the north. After a half hour of hard driving, he was sure that his pursuers had been suckered.

He exited the expressway and doubled back on surface streets to the exclusive residential suburb known as Uggijobi halfway between downtown Seoul and Pukhansan-Song National Park to the north.

Song-la Terrace was a quiet, tree-lined street where wide green hedges masked large houses with manicured lawns and formal gardens. The houses were large, white brick with red-tiled roofs. The only distinctively Oriental flavor was the red-painted wood on the windows and under the roof.

Carter found the number he wanted and swung in toward the wide iron gates. He smiled at the remote camera, and the gates swung open. Just inside was a small guardhouse built like a pagoda.

Carter guessed that the two men he saw inside were well armed.

He parked the car under an elaborately carved wooden overhang, and entered through a garden.

Kim Li met him at the door in an ultrafeminine black number that hugged her body like skin. A narrow silver belt highlighted her waist and a deeply cut bodice highlighted everything else. The dress was held by ridiculously thin silver straps across her shoulders, and bright red toenails peeked out from narrow-heeled silver sandals.

"Hi, going out for dinner?"

She one-upped him. "No, I thought we would dine in this evening. Would you like tea?"

"No. Whiskey, a double."

She made a face. "In here."

It was a large office-cum-living room. One entire wall was a giant fireplace of native stone that would gobble a good chunk of Sequoia on its huge grate. The rest was equally as opulent and lush: plum carpeting, rich paneling, low furniture in sand-colored leather and pale wood. Bookcases, built-in bar, cooling air that seemed to be scented with pine. In one corner was an intercom, tape dictation equipment, and through an open doorway a small office with noiseless typewriter, a plain desk, filing cabinets.

Carter had an idea that somewhere close by there would be a smaller version of the vast communications setup he had seen at Pak's palace in Hong Kong.

He hoped so. They were going to need it.

As Kim Li handed him the drink, she lightly touched the thick bandage on his head.

"It looks as though you have had a great deal of success or a great deal of failure."

"A little of both." He lit a cigarette, gathered his thoughts, and began. By the time he ran down, his glass was empty. She rescued it for a refill.

"Do you think you've done enough to convince them?" she asked.

"You mean, broach Bonner in his Pusan lair?"

"Yes."

He shook his head slowly. "No, not yet."

She glided back toward him with the drink in that way Oriental women have that gives a feeling that their legs are air and their feet don't touch the ground. He could almost hear the rustle of her legs moving against each other in the nylons.

"I'd like to nail one more spike to convince them," he said, taking the glass. "Are you still Pak's mistress?"

The shift in gears got to her. It brought a flush to her cheeks, but she rode over it and answered his question with a question. "What kind of spike do you need?"

"The sharpy in Big Mamma's who nailed me. He was good, damn good. He probably knows a lot of the story, right up to Bonner."

"But you said you don't know who he is."

"I don't. But I'll bet that bar girl does. With a little arm twisting or a little won—or both—I think I can get a name out of her."

"All the bar girls have to register with the police."

"I figured they did," Carter said. "Can you get pictures? I doubt if her real name is Suzy."

"I'll be back in a few minutes."

His voice stopped her at the door. "Without Kwon's people knowing?"

"Of course. We have our own sources."

She slipped from the room and Carter built a third drink. He was half asleep in the chair when she returned.

"Nick . . ."

"Ouch." She had squeezed his side.

"You're bandaged there, too?"

"Oh, yes," he groaned. "They had a good time. Got a spare bedroom?"

"Six of them. This way."

The bedroom looked as if it had been brought over from Versailles. The adjoining bath was equally as sumptuous.

"I'll take it," Carter said. "When can I move in?"

The quip finally got a laugh from her. She crossed to a huge armoire and opened the doors. "I brought a bag for you. These are all in your size. And, of course . . . these." She opened a drawer and Carter saw his hardware.

"Thanks. What time is dinner?"

"Whenever you want it."

"Nine. Wake me at eight."

She moved to the door as Carter headed for the bath.

"Nick . . ."

"Yeah?"

"In answer to your question . . . Mr. Pak gave up the joys of the flesh several years ago."

# NINE

The dinner was delicious, all traditional Korean dishes, with a double entree of *bulgalbi*, beef ribs, and *samyetang*, a whole small chicken cooked in a ginseng-flavored broth.

Carter devoured both plates and a bottle of rice wine as if he hadn't eaten for days. When he finished, he pushed the dessert away.

"Not one more bite. My compliments to the chef—he is a genius."

"I am the chef."

"My God . . ." Carter didn't finish. One of the shadows from the gate house appeared in the doorway, a manila envelope in his hand.

Carter was sorry for the interruption. From the look in Kim's eyes as she stood to fetch the envelope, she was too.

The shadow went back to his gate house and they moved into the office-living room with their coffee.

Kim slit the envelope and withdrew a stack of twelve large, glossy prints. One by one she started laying them out.

Carter stopped her at number seven. "That one."

"Her name is Soklay Jung. She lives at Twelve Sangdo-Chu. That would be in the new high-rise apartments south of the river. The apartment number is nine-eleven."

Carter glanced at his watch. It was nearly eleven. Figuring the girl would leave the bar at around two in the morning, he had plenty of time to get into her apartment before she got home.

He stood and stretched painfully. "I'll dress and pack a light bag." Suddenly he chuckled. "The luggage and clothing industry makes a fortune out of me."

"I'll change your body dressing."

He raised one eyebrow. "You're a doctor, too?"

She smiled enigmatically. "I am many things. Come."

Carter could sense it as he watched the movement of her body beneath the dress. At the top of the stairs he followed her into the room. With quick hands she removed his shirt.

He had tried to take a partial bath earlier. The thick bandage around his torso was wet. Deftly, Kim cut it away.

"I'll be right back."

She was gone almost five minutes. When she returned, she carried half a pharmacy in a small bag.

"Do you have much pain still?"

"Not much."

"Then it is better you take no pills that will dull your senses."

With expert fingers she cut away the old bandage and applied a new one. Carter couldn't tell the professionalism of the new from the old.

She glanced at his face. "Too tight?"

"No, fine," he replied. "You're good at this."

She shrugged. "Often the people who work for me have similar problems. It is best not to involve doctors." She studied the bandage around his head. "It would be less noticeable if I removed that and applied a smaller one. You could wear a hat."

"Go ahead."

Her body was close as she worked; the clean, female smell of her filled his nostrils. At last she held his face in her hands and studied the results. "Much better." She looked up at him and suddenly her face glowed.

"You're blushing."

"I know."

Carter bent slowly and touched his lips to hers. She responded at once, gliding her arms around his neck. Her tongue probed the inside of his mouth and her body moved slowly against his.

His hands slid down her body and over the curve of her hips.

"Wait," she whispered, and moved a step away.

She unfastened the dress with one movement of her hand. It shimmered to the floor, revealing the flowing perfection of her lithe figure. The wisp of her strapless bra followed. Her hands, palms flat, roamed down the length of her body and then the pantyhose were gone.

She returned to him. As her fingers worked at his belt, his hands explored the taut fullness of her breasts.

"You have many scars," she said, running her fingertips over his naked flesh.

"There have been many battles."

"Is everything all right?" she asked.

"Everything is fine," he smiled.

She sat on the bed and reached for him. Her hand closed around his wrist and pulled him down to her.

Her naked arms and jutting breasts were soft satin against his face. He kissed them. She moaned and her lips found his. Her tongue flickered tiny messages of desire into the sensitive parts of his mouth.

Carter forgot about Mr. Pak and Dr. Kwon and the rest of the night.

The skin of her naked body was soft, smooth and taut at the same time. He held her and kissed her throat as the hardened tips of her breasts teased his chest. His hands found her thighs and her breath quickened.

She twisted into him eagerly, and he groaned aloud.

"Your side?" she cried with alarm.

"My whole body," he laughed.

His laughter was genuine, and so was the tremendous sigh that escaped through his mouth when every part of his being surrendered to her caresses. Her face had become childishly innocent as she stared into his face and returned his laughter. Carter felt her hands work familiarly over his body.

Their laughter filled the room and turned into snickers, finally into heavy breathing and sighing. She sat astride his thighs and took him into her. Her head reared back; her eyes stared sightlessly above her. His sighs came up to greet hers.

"God," she moaned.

"Yes," he answered, and he felt her rocking, swaying buttocks rustle and slide against his flesh. Felt her muscles seize and possess him greedily.

They were two lusting animals at first, without restraint. Later, she caressed him softly until the tremors of passion coursed through them.

The rushing sensation of orgasm made her quiver and rock. Her body pulsated inside and out. She fell forward against him as he embraced her tightly. They lay together in the dark, their bodies growing quiet and calm. Carter caressed her back. The tenderness of the gesture made Kim's face go softer, more childlike.

"When must you go?" she whispered finally.

"Now."

It burst the bubble. Without a word, Kim slid off the bed and moved to the armoire to pack the bag he would take to Pusan.

Carter crossed the Han-Gang River on the iron bridge, and parked several blocks from the apartment house.

He skirted the whole building twice before approaching the entrance. He didn't expect any watchers, but he had already found out that Dr. Kwon had long arms.

The building was new, the clone of a dozen others on either side. There was no doorman and the outer doors were not locked.

On the ninth floor he found her apartment and, just in case, knocked.

There was no reply. He put his ear to the door and heard the sound of loudly running water in another room. He picked the door lock, pushed the door open, and entered.

He stood in a comfortable living room, furnished tastefully with low Oriental furniture and hangings on the walls. He closed the door behind him, quietly.

He held the Luger ready in his right hand. Crossing the room carefully, he looked through a doorway. There was a bedroom, with a pastel wallpaper of Oriental design. On the bed was recently discarded clothing . . . slacks, a silk blouse, stockings, two scraps of feminine underclothing. Through a second doorway across the bedroom, the sound of the running water sounded like a small waterfall.

Soklay Jung was taking a shower.

Carter holstered the Luger and returned to the living room. Quietly and methodically he searched the place. A small desk, the drawers of an occasional table, a magazine rack. There was nothing of importance to him except a photograph, in a desk drawer, of a bald Caucasian and a dark-haired girl standing together on a beach, in bathing suits. There was an inscription on the face of the photo that read *To Soklay, from her Colonel*.

Carter took a long look at Soklay's face in the photograph and then replaced it in the drawer. He heard the water shut off in the shower, and then a small sound in the bathroom. He went to the open doorway and saw her just walking into the bedroom from the bath, dripping wet and completely naked.

She spotted him and gasped. "What are you doing here?" she sputtered.

Carter moved closer until he towered over her. "Did you know they beat me up?"

Her eyes dropped to the carpet. "Yes. I . . . I am sorry. I did not know they would do that."

"You know Tomiko Mochiko, don't you."

She winced, clutching the towel in an attempt to cover her nakedness. "Please, go away."

"I won't hurt you, I promise. Talk to me, and I swear to you no one will know of it."

She looked back up, her eyes narrowed. Her wet hair, falling down long over her shoulders and back, clung to her glistening flesh.

"I knew Tomiko. Like me, she was bar girl. But she is gone now."

"Where?"

"I do not know. But I know she works for Dr. Kwon. You are American. You do not know of Dr. Kwon. He is very powerful man in Korea."

"Where is she?"

"I do not know."

He clutched her shoulders with an iron grip. "Are you telling me the truth?"

"I am, I swear!"

He released her. "All right, let's try something else. The tall man, the one who led the others who beat me up. Who is he?"

She tried to bolt for the door, but he caught her and pulled her back. They struggled, his hands on her slippery flesh. Then he got a good hold on her and dumped her unceremoniously on the Western-style bed. He held her shoulders down and put his knees between her thighs.

"No, please!" There was real terror in her eyes.

"What is his name?" Carter hissed.

The fight went out of her. Carter released her and let her sit up on the bed. She gave up trying to hide her nudity.

"His name is Booja Dok. He is very mean man. He runs many things in Seoul for Dr. Kwon. Even police are afraid of Booja Dok."

"Where can I find him?"

She tensed again and then rose from the bed. Casually, she picked up a short skirt from a nearby chair and wriggled into it, making everything move at once. Now her hips were covered, but that was all. She made no effort to cover her torso. Carter saw that she was now relaxed. She lit a long cigarette and stood facing him, her breasts still damp from the shower.

"Two of the men were back in the bar tonight, the men who beat on you. I heard them talking. You ran away from them?"

Carter nodded. "At the airport."

"Then you must be very brave."

"And very mean. Probably much meaner than Booja Dok. Tell me where I can find him."

"He has a house, but he won't be there tonight."

"Then where would he be?"

"I heard the men say that he was sleeping with his

woman tonight. If you were found, they were to contact him there."

"Do you know the house of his mistress?"

She blew smoke out through one of her nostrils and succeeded in looking about ten years older than her true age.

"Booja has a brother. He runs a sex shop in the Pogwangdong. Booja owns the shop. Much dope is sold there. It is open all night."

"And the brother can tell me where I can find Booja?"

"I did not say that, did I?"

Carter dropped some bills on the bed from the fresh supply he had gotten from Kim Li. At the door, he paused and turned back.

"Soklay Jung, if Booja Dok is waiting for me, I will have to kill him. Then I will have to return here and kill you."

The store windows were almost painted over with lewd advertisements about what could be found inside. Through a small, clear space, he could see a man moving around inside.

Entering, Carter shuffled humbly toward a squat, chunky man who smirked at him over a flyspecked display case.

"Good evening, sir," Carter said. The man nodded. "I understand you are the brother of Booja Dok." The narrow eyes got narrower, but he nodded again. "I have been to Booja's house tonight for business. He was not there. He stays with his woman, I understand."

The man shrugged. "I would not know."

Carter went to the door and locked it. He pulled the blinds and flipped off the outside light.

As he went back to the counter, the man's eyes glided

over him, marking everything. Carter's size and strength, the stubborn set of his jaw, the hang of the sports jacket over the shoulder rig and the Luger.

Carter stared back, seeing a bigger than average Oriental, a man with a too-wise mouth and ropelike muscled shoulders.

"What are you called?"

"Kai."

"Kai Dok?" Carter said.

"Perhaps, sir, if you would give me your hotel—"

Carter braced his hands under the edge of the heavy glass countertop. It tilted and the man leaped out of the way as it crashed on its side, spewing glass and dildos in every direction.

"Well?" Carter said again.

The Korean tried one of his brother's tricks, off the edge of the counter, his feet flashing toward the Killmaster's head.

But this time there was no surprise.

Carter caught him with his left hand locking around his throat. At the same time, he hit him just above the heart with all the power in his shoulder. After a second blow, this one wrist-deep in Kai's gut, Carter dragged him farther toward the back of the store away from any inquiring eyes.

The man gasped for breath, his face contorted with pain and rage. He was hunched over, his hands fumbling at the flesh over his heart, kneading away the pain.

"I am not bound by rules," Carter growled. "I will kill you, Kai, do you hear? I will break your neck in less than a minute if you do not tell me all I want to know."

The hand moved under his shirt and came out with a knife in a deft backhand movement, reaching high for Carter's throat. Carter had been watching the hand that held it; Kai had been rubbing his rib cage with that hand, or pretending to.

Rolling to his right, Carter felt the sharp whisper of air as the blade flicked past. The point chipped a sliver from the wooden wall. Kai tried to bring the knife back for a return swipe. Carter slammed the heels of both hands violently against a table edge and drove the flimsy top into Kai's belly. Then he leaned against the off-angled swing of the knife and chopped both hands to Kai's head.

The man fell, but hung on to the knife. Squirming like a crippled snake, he reached up at Carter with it. He should have let go of the blade when he had a chance, because Carter lifted the table and used it to hammer Kai's head lopsided.

"Stop, stop . . ."

Kai was swimming between death and semiconsciousness when Carter stopped.

"*Where*?" he hissed.

"Number Ten Kwana No, in Shillim-dong. Please . . ."

Carter slammed him once more with the table leg, dropped it, and walked out of the shop.

# TEN

The street was quiet, the houses old-style Korean and far apart. Carter glided the car past a mangy dog sniffing for scraps of food.

He spotted the house and drove a few blocks past it. After parking, he doubled back off the road.

He was far south of the city here. He could smell farm animals and the rank odor of manure freshly spread in the rice paddies.

Behind the houses he found a narrow footpath. He followed it slowly to keep from slipping into the knee-deep brown muck that filled the rice paddy to his right. He had slipped several times already, and his legs and shoes were covered with the fertilized slime. The main road was an elevated shadow on his left.

He reached the end of the houses, number 18, and started counting down. Between 11 and 10, he paused and moved to the rear windows.

Silence and not a light on.

Soundlessly, he moved back to the front door. The street

was still deserted. He could only hope that there was no insomniac staring out his window.

He had his picks in hand and a quick inspection of the lock told him that only two could possibly fit. The second one did it, and he went quickly in past a tiny vestibule with a scatter rug and a small table backed by a mirror. The stairs went straight up to a landing and another door, and the second key unlocked that.

There was a small hall here with a dining room on the left and the living room on the right. The furniture, all but the overstuffed divan and chairs, was Korean, occasional tables, a low chest, the lamp bases. The Oriental rugs on the waxed hardwood floors looked authentic, and after his first look he went to an inner hall and found it led to two bedrooms and two baths, one room unmistakably feminine and the other monastic in its simplicity.

He decided that Booja Dok's woman might live in a lousy neighborhood in a so-so house, but he hadn't spared any expense in making the interior comfortable.

He doubled back to the larger bedroom and quietly opened the door. Beads of moonlight slanted across their bodies on the bed.

Booja Dok had good taste. The woman was tall for a Korean, and surprisingly buxom.

The Killmaster moved to the side of the bed and laid the Luger along the man's belly. When the eyes opened, Carter got a handful of hair and lifted his head so he could see where the gun was pointed.

"Struggle or make a sound and I'll blow your dick into next week."

The woman did exactly as she was told. When Dok was tied up with her panty hose, Carter did the same for her. Then he gagged her.

"What do you do?" Dok asked.

"Take you someplace quiet," Carter replied, "where you can scream."

He laid the barrel of the Luger along the side of the Korean's head and went to get the rental.

When he returned, Booja Dok was awake enough to have struggled to his feet.

*He's a tough son of a bitch*, Carter thought, swinging the automatic. The Luger caught him at the base of the skull, and that did it. The body sagged slackly, then fell and lay heaped against the wall.

Carter moved behind the man, twisted up a handful of the long hair, pulled his head back, and drove his fist straight into his face. The nose went and some teeth sheared off at the gums.

Carter let him fall. He waited a moment, looking down at Dok lying on his back, and when it was obvious he lay absolutely unconscious, Carter dragged him from the house and dumped him in the trunk of the rental.

He drove on the main road for an hour toward the mountains to the east. When Dok started kicking the inside of the trunk lid, Carter pulled into a cutout and parked under some trees. Taking a flashlight from the glove compartment, he went around to the rear of the car. He opened the trunk and Dok glared up into the light.

"Listen and listen good," Carter hissed. "I'm heading east into the mountains along the coast. When I find a nice, quiet place, we're going to have a long talk. If you don't want to stay quiet until I get to this nice quiet place, I'll dump you out here and put a bullet in the back of your head. *Nae?*"

When he got no answer, Carter planted his fist in his gut. *"Nae?"*

The man hawked and gagged and drew great heaving breaths like a runner collapsing across the finish line.

But he managed to nod.

Carter slammed the lid and got back in the car. He drove into the mountains until he could see no lights for miles around, and then turned off on a narrow, rutted lane.

Now he killed the headlights and slowed to a crawl. The moon was down, but it was clear and stars shone, so the twin pale tracks on either side of the grassy middle hump of the road weren't hard to follow. But the light was too poor to move fast, and Carter couldn't afford to drag the oil pan on high center and hole it.

The water-cut ravines became more frequent and the trees more sparse the higher he climbed.

Then he was on a climbing track, close under the dark shapes of high peaks that rose to almost obliterate the sky. He dropped into a pass and knew it was safe to turn on his headlights. He could no longer be seen from the main road.

He crept along the narrow, winding, ever-higher road, topping the first crest inside the pass and dropping down into a wide park. The road got rougher, chuckholed. Several times he had to stop, get out, and remove dead trees or rocks from the way.

Then he came over a rise and saw what he had been looking for, a ranger's hut. A month from now it would be inhabited. But now, with the snow recently melted, there was little chance for fires in the vast park.

It took him the better part of an hour to wind around the peak to the hut with the low-slung car. With a Jeep he could have made it in minutes.

He stopped, grabbed the flashlight, and went into the hut. In a second he could see that it hadn't been used since the previous fall. Dust lay thick on the floor crisscrossed with tracks of rats, mice, and insects.

Satisfied, he went back to the car. He unlocked the trunk and rolled Dok out onto the ground. Grabbing the panty hose that secured the Korean's ankles to his wrists and the wrists to another pair around his neck, Carter dragged the man into the hut.

"Who are you?" It was practically the first thing Booja Dok had said since Carter had rousted him out of his mistress's bed.

"I, my friend, am a very pissed-off man."

Carter activated the spring in Hugo's sheath and the hilt of the stiletto settled into his palm. The Korean's eyes grew wide as he saw light glint on the blade. When the flashlight was propped on a rough wood table for illumination, Carter turned Dok over.

With his knee in the man's back, he slit the pajamas down the back and peeled him. This done, he flipped him over and propped him up against the wall. Then he gave him a light tap with the muzzle of the Luger, chopping it across the swollen lump at the base of the man's skull.

"You ready for our little chat now?"

Dok spit, just enough to hit Carter's shoe.

Carter ground the Luger harder into the side of his neck. "I sold a guy named Toby Sukimoto some very advanced electronics parts for a great deal of money. I know they found their way to Korea. I figure Sukimoto sold 'em to someone else here. I want my money."

Silence.

"Since you and your buddies beat the shit out of me last night, I figure you must know that someone else, who that buyer is." He tapped him again lightly with the Luger.

Suddenly Dok spit again and a stream of curses erupted from his lips in staccato Korean.

"Okay, tough guy."

Carter jacked a round into the chamber of the Luger, sighed, and shot him through the calf of the right leg. It was just enough to groove the muscle so it bled profusely but not dangerously.

"I will bleed to death!" Dok screamed.

"Maybe," Carter said. "You got any more remarks about my mother and what I can do to her and myself?"

The big shoulders sagged a bit. "Tomiko Mochiko is a hostess at the Empire casino in Pusan."

"The only casino I know in Pusan is at the Paradise Beach Hotel."

"The Empire is an illegal casino, by invitation only."

"Now we're getting somewhere. Who owns it?"

"I don't know."

Carter suddenly reached forward and jammed the Luger's muzzle against Dok's smashed nose. The man howled and tears of pain flowed from his swollen eyes.

"Who owns this casino?" Carter barked, moving to Dok's side and screwing the muzzle of the gun into his ear.

"Jacques Bonner."

"Who does Bonner work for?"

"Dr. Kwon."

"Who the hell is Dr. Kwon?" Carter growled, grinding.

"I don't know. No one knows. If I did know, and I told you, I would be dead."

"You asshole," Carter hissed, "what the hell do you think this is, a popgun? I've already shot you once."

The man's head fell forward to his chest. "Then you will have to kill me. I do not know Dr. Kwon."

"Who do you take your orders from?"

"Bonner."

Of course Carter already knew everything he had been told, but information wasn't the reason for this little exercise. Fear, intimidation, and getting Dr. Kwon's attention was.

He figured that had been accomplished. But he remained quiet, not moving or uttering a word.

The silence in the hut stretched out until it had substance of its own. The world has become so noisy that utter silence such as found in remote mountains in the dead of night has a fearful, oppressing effect, as though the night without sound bred fear.

Finally Dok couldn't take it. He looked up and Carter gave him his meanest leer.

Dok couldn't meet Carter's eyes. He finally settled on the gun still pointed at his head.

"Are you going to kill me?"

"I haven't decided."

"You should," Dok said, his eyes pools of dark hate.

"Why?"

"Because if you let me live, I will find you. And when I find you, I will peel the skin from your body."

Carter laughed long and hard. He stood, grabbed the flashlight, and headed for the door.

"Don't leave me here!" Dok screamed.

Carter kept going.

"I will kill you!"

"Good luck," Carter shot back over his shoulder, and climbed into the car.

As he drove out of the mountains toward the coastal road that would take him south toward Pusan, he felt total satisfaction.

Between demolishing the sex shop and terrorizing the Dok brothers, Dr. Kwon and Jacques Bonner would surely know that Carter was around.

*And they will surely know that I am a bad-ass to deal with when the time comes.*

# ELEVEN

In his entire life, Jacques Bonner had been afraid of nothing. No man or woman had ever cracked his impenetrable shield. Not even death frightened him.

Until his greed had caused him to entwine his future with Dr. Kwon.

Jacques Bonner feared Dr. Kwon. And this fear became almost paralyzing when the well-oiled machine Kwon had created and Bonner ran came up against obstacles.

"Well?"

"The goods have been recovered," Bonner replied. "It was an easy matter to find out who Kyo hired to do the hijacking. The components were recovered in Inchon."

Dr. Kwon inhaled deeply and let the smoke return to the room in two perfect streams from his nostrils. "The thieves?"

"Dead. Their bodies will never be found. I think Kyo was struck dumb when he found out what the shipment was. He didn't know how to handle it, sell it. That was why he tried to get back in our good graces by informing on his conspirators."

Kwon smiled. "Had the shipment been the fruit of the poppy, Kyo would have known exactly what to do with it. He is back in Pusan?"

Bonner nodded. "So is Ho Shan. He is devising a scheme now to do away with Kyo."

"Be sure that it would appear as an accident. A K-CIA agent is not a common thug. His death must be in the line of duty. What else?"

Bonner was sweating, debating with himself if he should make a decision on the next problem himself.

"Jacques, what else? My tea is getting cold and your whores are probably impatient."

"It's this American, Nicholas Crider."

"The one who wants us to pay for Sukimoto's last shipment?"

Bonner nodded. "I checked in the states. It's impossible to track down all of Toby Sukimoto's suppliers. This Crider could be one. Then again, maybe he's just a shakedown artist."

"Jacques, you're nervous, sweating. Didn't Dok and his people take care of this man?"

"Not exactly."

Bonner related all the details. He told Kwon about the sex shop, and this man Crider leaving Dok on the mountain. Kwon accepted it much better than Bonner would have expected. There was actually a smile on the thin, arrogant lips.

"This Crider would seem to be a persistent fellow, and nervy."

"According to Dok, he is probably here in Pusan by now. Should we find him and take care of the problem ourselves?"

"Yes, but send for Dok. Let him finish the job. If he should fail twice, he is no longer of any use to us."

"That is all for now," Bonner said.

"We will meet with the North Koreans in four days' time. Make sure everything is ready."

"I will."

Dr. Kwon stood and moved like a graceful shadow from the room.

Jacques Bonner took a handkerchief from his lapel pocket and mopped his forehead.

In Pusan, Carter headed for the railroad depot plaza. It was directly in the center of the city and within easy walking distance to the two main areas where he guessed he would be doing much of his business.

Texas Town was an area of brothels, bars, and nightclubs ranging from classy to raunchy. Whatever the itch, it could be scratched in Texas Town.

Nombumin-dong was the port area where the fishing fleet was tied up and where the fish market, scores of restaurants, and more nightlife was located.

Carter guessed that somewhere between the two he would find the Empire Casino.

He had to hit only three bars before he got a name: Hun Wook, "the man who makes arrangements."

The area was on the edge of Texas Town toward the docks: bars side by side, restaurants, curio shops, street hawkers, one-man noodle stands on wheels, milling crowds of pickpockets and pimps.

Hun Wook owned the building in which he lived and worked, as well as the land and all the other structures on, in, and under the entire block. One of his minor investments.

Getting in to see Wook was not difficult. The man was in the people business. He was the go-between. He bought and sold information, placed and took bribes; he received and passed on messages, or answered them himself. Carter had only to state his business as "personal and of a rather delicate nature," and he was passed into the throne room when his turn came.

Wook was like so many men of his chosen profession. He was quite short, even for a Korean. He was dark, his eyes were hazel, and he had most of his hair, but he was self-conscious about losing it, because he'd let it grow long on the left side and had it carefully plastered across the balding spots. He wore gold-framed eyeglasses, and when he shook hands it was as though Carter took hold of a damp, limp, lifeless small paw.

Wook gestured toward a chair. "Sit down, please, Mr. . . . ah"—he looked at a note his secretary handed over when Carter was allowed into the room—"ah, Crider. Is that correct?"

"Yes."

"Ah, yes!" Wook shook his head and smiled. He had gold around the edge of one tooth. "Now, of what service may I be to you?"

Carter didn't say anything. He stared at the man, waiting. Wook simply returned the stare, and Carter thought, *He's a cool little creep. He knows heat and how to handle it. He hasn't spent all his life behind a desk too large for him and he's made some fundamental adjustments . . . like he didn't make me sit while he stood, so he could look me in the eyes on his level instead of having to look up. Being small doesn't bother him because he knows how powerful he is otherwise.*

"If you please, Mr. Crider, I have others waiting, some of them on urgent business. But I have a rule and have never broken it . . . I see people in their turn, in the precise order they come to my office. But you must state your business, sir, or leave at once and let me get on with mine."

"You know who I am, don't you."

"Only that your name is Crider, and that your business is personal, and of a delicate nature." Wook smiled. "I would suppose you want an abortion for some young woman, as an offhand guess. It can be arranged." He snapped his fingers. "Two hundred dollars cash in advance. It is no problem, and the price includes my fee."

"The word is out on Nicholas Crider and you got it. That's all right. I expected it. I was looking for a Japanese broad named Tomiko Mochiko. Now I've got another name, two in fact... and a place. I think you know them both already."

Wook shrugged.

"The place is the Empire Casino. I am told that one has to be referred in order to gain admittance."

"If such a casino existed, I am sure it would be primarily for Koreans..."

His voice trailed off and he leaned back in his chair, steepling his fingers, looking up at the bookcase covering the wall to Carter's left. "You mentioned names."

"Jacques Bonner and someone called Dr. Kwon."

Hun Wook leaned forward and placed his elbows on the table. "What do you hope to accomplish, Mr. Crider?"

"I want to collect two hundred and fifty thousand dollars that is owed to me. If you act as my introduction to Bonner, ten percent is yours."

Carter could sense from the man's smile that he thought Carter was an idiot. But that was all right. Wook would contact Bonner, and there was an outside chance that he would be able to get inside the casino through the front door.

There were chances, of course, that several other things

could happen, but Carter had prepared himself for everything.

"For such a sum of money, Mr. Crider, I will most certainly see what I can do. Excuse me for a few moments, if you will."

The few moments turned into nearly an hour before he returned to the office, beaming. "Mr. Bonner will be most happy to sit down and talk with you. The Empire Casino is located in the Nampo-dong amusement area. The address is on this paper. Any taxi driver can take you there."

Carter stood. "We will be in touch."

"I sincerely hope so, sir."

Again Carter took the limp hand, and left the office. At the edge of Texas Town, he bypassed two taxis who cruised him, and caught a third.

"Yes, sir?"

"This address," Carter said, and showed the man the paper that Wook had given him.

The driver shrugged and dropped the flag. "Very much traffic tonight. Better to take smaller streets. All right with you, sir?"

"Whatever," Carter said.

They drove for about twenty minutes before the traffic thinned to a trickle so Carter could spot the tail. It was an older model Renault sedan.

They were on a quiet side street now, the driver avoiding the heavy traffic of the boulevard that paralleled them. Carter turned and looked out the rear window again, and saw the black Renault sedan only a half block behind them and closing.

"How long has that car been behind us?" he said to the driver.

"Sir?"

"The car!" Carter snapped. "Behind us!"

The driver glanced in the rearview mirror. "Ah. Yes, a car."

Carter made an ugly sound in his throat and curled the fingers of his left hand around the back of the driver's neck. "You son of a bitch, you're with 'em, aren't you?"

"I don't know what you say."

"I'm no expert on Pusan, but I think the Nampo-dong amusement area is about eight miles in the other direction."

Now the driver was visibly shaken. Carter could feel him shaking clear through his neck, and the collar of his shirt was suddenly soaked through with sweat.

"Turn right at this next corner!" Carter barked, pulling the Luger but keeping it low behind the seat.

The driver glanced again through the rearview mirror at the Renault, his eyes fearful. Carter was sure now that the driver was either one of them or he and several other drivers had been paid to take Carter in a certain direction to a certain place no matter who picked him up.

He flicked off the Luger's safety. It was time to let Jacques Bonner know just how nasty he could get.

The driver was hesitating, weighing his chances of survival with Carter or the occupants of the Renault.

"Turn, you bastard!" Carter ground the muzzle of the Luger in the man's ear to help him to a decision.

The driver made a hard right turn, tires squealing. The driver of the Renault gave up the pretense of holding back, and came around the corner with his own tires screaming.

"Turn left," Carter hissed, "and drive faster!"

He did, and the black car followed, right on their tail. The taxi driver started to accelerate, but the Renault pulled around to the left quickly and came up alongside. Carter could see the faces in the other car, three of them. The driver of the Renault turned hard into the taxi and there was a crashing and rending of metal.

The taxi driver swore and almost lost control of the cab. It went up onto the curb and barely missed a couple walking on a dusty sidewalk. The driver got control again.

Carter aimed the Luger and fired at the driver of the other car. The Renault bounced and swerved and his aim went wild, but the slug hit the neck of the man riding beside the driver. He jerked limply and then his mouth flew open and he fell onto the driver. The driver pushed him away and crashed again into the taxi. This time the taxi went up and over the sidewalk and smashed into a building front and bounced back to the curb, where it slammed into a utility pole.

Carter was thrown into the front seat, where his back and head jammed up against the dash. The taxi driver hit the windshield with his face, but not before the steering wheel had crushed his chest in on his heart and lungs. There was an accompanying explosion of sound, with metal and wood and glass all shrieking under the impact, and then the car was motionless, the radiator hissing steam.

Carter raised his bruised body and aimed the Luger toward the other car, which had pulled to a stop just beyond the utility pole. The two remaining men jumped out and ran in a crouch toward him. He fired off another shot at the closest man and the gunman yelled, his arms flying outward, his legs moving in different directions until he thumped onto the pavement, pooling blood beneath him.

The last man was hobbling. Light from a streetlight bathed his face for a second before he slid behind it for cover.

It was Booja Dok.

"Well, well, Dok," Carter yelled, putting an aching, groaning rasp in his voice, "have you come to peel my skin?"

"Come out of there, and I will not kill you!" Dok

shouted at the shattered windshield that obscured his view of Carter.

Crouched like a leopard in the front seat of the taxi, the Luger held up beside his right temple ready for use, Carter let a hard grin tickle the very edge of his straight-lined mouth.

"Do you hear me?" Dok shouted. "Drop your gun and come out!"

Down the street, several heads had appeared at doorways and were bent curiously in their direction.

"You must be injured! I will give you medical help!" Dok called, air hissing through his teeth.

Carter held the gun down lower. "All right. I'm out of ammunition. My right arm is busted. I'm finished."

"Throw your gun out of the car," Dok said in a hard voice.

Carter had been afraid of that. He glanced quickly around the taxi, and saw a heavy clipboard on the seat beside the dead driver. He picked it up and slipped it out the door on his side, the side away from the utility pole and Dok. It clattered to the pavement and the sound was very like that of a small gun.

Behind the pole, Dok craned his neck to see what Carter had thrown out, but could not. He hesitated, then stepped out from behind the pole and walked carefully to the driver's side of the taxi, the gun held out in front of him. He saw the dead driver, and then Carter's head, where he was crouched on the other side of the car.

"Well. That is very good, very smart. Now get to your feet slowly and—"

Carter raised the Luger in an unhurried way, aimed it carefully while Dok's eyes changed, and fired. The slug hit Dok just over the heart and pushed him backward away from the window of the car, hitting him like a club and sprawling him in the dusty street.

Carter got out of the cab and came around into the street to have a look. Dok was all twisted up on the cobbled pavement, the gun still in his hand. His gun hand twitched once, but he was dead.

Quickly, Carter darted from body to body. He collected everything from their pockets and rolled it up in the taxi driver's jacket.

Within two minutes after killing Dok, he was running as hard as he could down a side street toward a sign that said Underground in Korean.

He took the first train two stops, and came back up to street level. He walked a block and darted into a fish market that was just closing.

The old woman in the market thought he was crazy paying a thousand won for a plastic bag.

Back on the street, he dumped the contents of the jacket into the plastic bag and discarded the jacket in a street waste receptacle.

Three blocks farther on, he found another taxi and showed him the address on the paper.

"I know this address is in the Nampo-dong area," he hissed. "If you do not take me directly to the Nampo-dong area, I will pound your ass so far through that seat it will be dragging on the street. Do you understand?"

"*Ye*," the driver said, and dropped the meter with a look at Carter that said, *You are a crazy man!*

# TWELVE

There was no mistaking the Nampo-dong area when they reached it. Beer halls, *soju* bars, and tearooms were jammed cheek-to-jowl with little specialty stores crammed with every kind of merchandise imaginable.

The cab turned in from a well-lighted plaza and nosed down between bumper-to-bumper cars parked for the night on both sides of the narrow one-way street. When they stopped, the driver grunted and pointed to a sign above a dark doorway.

That's about all he had done in the wild ride across town: grunt occasionally, whistle through his teeth, and throw puzzled glances at Carter in the rearview mirror.

Carter got out, paid him with a heavy tip, and waited until the taxi had chugged off down the street.

The Killmaster moved into a dark stairwell and lit a cigarette. In the ten minutes it took to smoke it, he saw three cars disgorge well-dressed, laughing couples. Each of them entered the doorway across the street and climbed the dimly lit stairs.

He had the right place.

He tossed the butt of the cigarette into the gutter, tied a knot in the top of the plastic bag, and crossed the street.

On the second landing, he ran into a beefy type with a plastered-on smile that didn't match the frown in his eyes. The tuxedo he wore was expensive, but it looked as if he had gained about forty pounds after buying it.

"Good evening, sir."

"I don't speak Korean," Carter replied. "Japanese?"

"Yes, sir. What can I do for you?"

"Hun Wook sent me over," Carter replied, smiling and holding out the bag. "To deliver this personally to Mr. Bonner."

The pretense of a smile disappeared and the frown deepened. "I am afraid that is impossible, sir. I would be glad to take it to Mr. Bonner for you."

"Of course."

Carter retreated around the corner of the hallway and waited until he heard the door open and close. Quickly, pulling his lockpicks from his pocket, he ran to the door. The second try got it and he darted inside.

A cute little girl in a skintight dress with slits in the sides up to her black panties came through a curtain behind a counter.

"Good evening, sir, may I help you?"

She looked puzzled at seeing a "round-eye," but probably figured the muscle in the tuxedo had passed him through.

"I'm here to see Mr. Bonner," Carter said, and breezed on into the casino.

The room was large, with Eastern and Western games of chance galore. The clientele were mostly Asian, with a few visiting Western VIPs. Carter figured about a hundred and fifty people spreading over three rooms. The men were neatly dressed in well-tailored silk suits with a tuxedo here and there, the women in cocktail dresses or long gowns, all looking very elegant and expensive.

There was a long buffet table set up in one of the rooms, covered with platters of canapés, cold meats, beautifully prepared seafoods and salads, and waiters circulated with excellent champagne on silver trays. Carter spotted Moët, Dom Perignon, Veuve Cliquot, and a very good Bolinger '59. They even had it served in tulip-shaped glasses.

There was Haig and Haig scotch, Old Granddad bourbon, Booths and Gordon's gin, and a vodka Carter had never heard of but which was distilled and bottled in Russia. The cognacs were Courvoisier and Rémy Martin. Lined up on the glass-topped bar was the best array of red Bordeaux and Burgundy wines he'd ever seen assembled in one place. An equally extraordinary selection of whites were in silver ice buckets, and it occurred to him that whatever the future might hold for him personally, he was going to enjoy at least part of the evening.

All in all, Jacques Bonner ran a very classy, if illegal, place.

Carter got a glass of fine champagne at the bar, which was free, and moved to one of three roulette tables.

The croupier looked as puzzled as the bartender and checkroom girl, but traded won chips for the five one-hundred-dollar bills Carter fanned out.

He played black and won, red and won, and put the four-hundred on 13. Out of the corner of his eye he saw Muscles in the tuxedo hurry to the front door. He exited and popped back through. He spoke to the checkroom girl, and then roamed the room with his eyes.

The ball was spinning as he hotfooted it toward Carter.

"Excuse me, sir . . ."

"Yeah?"

"Would you follow me, please?"

"No," Carter said with a smile as the little ball dropped into the 13 slot. "Not right now. I'm winning."

The croupier shoved a huge stack of very high denomination chips toward Carter, and he pushed them over to black.

"If you don't follow me, sir, I will have to take you."

"You can try," Carter said, "but by the time you do, three or four of these tables will be wrecked and some of your fancy customers might get caught in the middle."

"Black."

Carter moved the whole pile to red while Muscle tensed and fumed at his elbow. The ball spun again.

"Red."

Carter pocketed all but one large chip and placed it on double-0. "You'd better tell Bonner to invite me personally before I break this joint."

The big man tensed a little more, frustration all over his face, and lumbered away.

Carter continued to play, winning the big ones and losing the small ones, and a crowd began to gather. They were getting a charge out of someone beating the house, and enthusiastically urged him on.

When the double-0 hit on Carter's third try around, a whoop went up. A stately old Korean gentleman dressed all in white, which made him a venerable grandpa who didn't have to work anymore, wanted to buy Carter's system.

All of a sudden Carter noticed that things began to quiet down. His circle of new friends started to thin out, and it wasn't because they were tired of seeing him win.

"Mr. Crider?" The voice was low, controlled, cold.

Carter picked up his latest stack of winnings and rolled his head to the side.

There was no mistaking the tall man at his elbow:

Jacques Bonner. Like the venerable old man, he wore a pure white suit and tie. But there was nothing old about Jacques Bonner. He was well over six feet, and even standing still he had the easy, lithe grace of a panther. His face was lean and patrician, the cheekbones high, the skin taut. It was the face of a man who habitually held himself in check. Only his mouth told a different story. It was full and sensuous, hinting at a dual nature in which frequent clashes were inevitable.

He held out his hand. "Jacques Bonner. I believe you wanted to see me?"

The thin smile over his white teeth wasn't in his eyes. Carter doubted if his eyes ever smiled. He was a man with no time to waste on smiling for anything but show.

His grip was like steel and Carter returned it in kind. "Yes, a gentleman from Seoul referred me to you . . . under duress."

The flinch was slight, barely noticeable, around the eyes. "My office is this way."

He led, with Carter in the middle and Muscles in the rear. They went upstairs to the third floor and through a pair of solid wooden doors marked Private in Korean.

It was an outer office, probably for a secretary. A huge desk was cluttered with unopened mail. The In basket was full and the one marked Out was empty. Wooden filing cabinets, without a single scratch on the varnish, were along one wall.

Whoever the secretary was, Carter thought, she rarely worked.

Two more double doors led to the inner office. It was much larger and almost lavish. There was a fine, carved teak desk with a glass top, a leather chair and sofa, tasteful paintings on the wall, deep pile carpeting, and leaded windows.

All very comfortable and elegant.

Spread across the desk were the contents of the plastic bag.

Bonner moved behind the desk and faced Carter. "Are you armed?"

"Yes."

Bonner shrugged and sat down, motioning for Carter to take the opposite chair. He ran his hand across the wallets and other articles Carter had taken off the three men.

"Fairly impressive calling card."

Carter lit a cigarette. "I wasn't too impressed with their owners."

The lips twisted into, for Bonner, the semblance of a smile. "Obviously, you, Crider, are becoming one very large pain in the ass."

"It doesn't take much to get me off your back, Mr. Bonner."

"Oh?"

Carter took the chips he had won from his pockets and stacked them on the desk. Quickly he added them up to around fifteen thousand once they were converted into American dollars.

"With this, I figure you owe me only a little over two hundred grand."

"You're out of your bloody mind."

Carter kept smiling, kept his voice low and controlled as he leaned across the desk. Out of the corner of his eye he saw Muscles in the tuxedo push away from the door a couple of steps.

"Look, Bonner, I don't give a damn who you are or what you do. A guy named Toby Sukimoto bought some very expensive goods from me in the States. He didn't pay. I try to find his girl friend. I figure she knows who took delivery or where the goods are. You follow me so far?"

The ice-blue eyes flicked once to the beefy bouncer and back to Carter. Then he nodded.

"Okay. While I'm looking for the girl, a punk named Booja Dok tries to rearrange my bones. He tells me to forget my money and leave Korea. Now, that makes me very pissed-off. I do a number on this Booja Dok, and your name pops up. You know what I suddenly think? I think maybe you're the one with my goods. So maybe I ought to collect from you."

It was hardly a movement, a mere flicker of one eyelid, but it was like a spring in the rear of the two-hundred-pound bouncer.

He came around with both hands fisted like a hammer. If it had connected, it would have taken off Carter's head.

It didn't come close to connecting.

Carter rolled off the chair to the side, taking with him a steel paperweight gilded like a bar of gold. It weighed a little over a pound and Carter figured it would stop a bull, applied in the right place.

He used his legs for springs and came over the chair before the Korean could get his balance. He caught the Korean with two vicious blows, one on top of the head and one on his left ear.

The man turned out to be more than a bull. He shook his head and made a grab for Carter. The Killmaster backed away and swung the paperweight in his right hand in roundhouse swings.

The Korean, blinded and maddened with pain, just kept coming. Carter hit him at least eight more times before the man's knees started to buckle.

His left ear was swelling up like a sausage. One of the blows had torn part of it loose, and he was spattering blood like a garden hose, and still trying to get at Carter. It was silent in the room except for the wet sounds of the steel bar and the Korean's grunts of pain. Carter didn't want to kill him, but he had to stop him. If Muscles got him by the throat, the Killmaster knew it would be all over. He'd hang on no matter how hard Carter kneed him in the groin.

He was as tall as Carter, so the Killmaster had to stand on his toes to deliver a last blow. Up he went and down whistled the bar. It caught him squarely on the top of the head. A less thick-skulled man would probably have died from it. The Korean didn't die, then or later, but the crack on the head stopped him cold. Bloody saliva dribbled from the corners of his mouth and his eyes glazed over as he crashed to the carpeted floor.

Carter moved out of the way as he fell. He didn't try to catch him. He just dropped the hunk of steel and moved his right hand toward the Luger.

There was no need. Bonner was leaning calmly against the edge of the desk, lighting a thin cigar and looking down at his man.

"Name's Rinn-Sup Jo. Good man, mean son of a bitch. Is he dead?"

Carter rolled him over with his toe. "Don't think so."

Bonner eyed him through the wreath of smoke around his head. "Just what kind of stuff did you sell Toby Sukimoto?"

Carter rattled off a list of components—hardware, software, micropackaging—most of what AXE knew was being sold illegally.

Bonner only nodded, but Carter could almost see his mind working.

"Where are you staying, Mr. Crider?"

"Nowhere, yet."

"I've got a house, in the hills up the coast. Be my guest for a couple of days?"

"What's in it for me?"

The broad shoulders rippled the white jacket. "Maybe you'll get what you say is owed you, and maybe you'll get more business."

"You got all the comforts of home in this house of yours?"

Bonner's laugh was hollow, like an echo in a well or dungeon. "If you mean booze and broads, I never sleep without 'em."

# THIRTEEN

Bonner's personal car was a Mercedes limo, a little less than a block long, complete with a driver and a second man riding shotgun.

They found Carter's car and the second man drove it.

The Killmaster expected conversation during the ride up the coast, but he got none. A little less than an hour after leaving the city, they turned away from the sea and Bonner pointed to a huge walled structure at the top of a commanding hill.

"Up there."

Carter could see only the high tile-topped stuccoed wall and the top of the house roof protruding above. But what he saw stood out in the pale moonlight like an ancient castle.

The car climbed up the steep paved drive and halted at a huge wooden gate. The chauffeur honked and the gate was opened by a girl in Chinese pajamas. When she saw who it was, she stepped aside and the car entered. Even in the darkness the view inside the wall took Carter's breath away. The house was a rambling, three-story affair that sat behind a landscaped garden of miniature trees that gave the illusion that the garden went on forever into an endless forest.

"Business must be good," Carter commented dryly.

"Business is very good," came the equally dry reply.

As the girl passed in front of the car's lights, Carter spotted a machine pistol slung across her back. "You have female watchdogs?"

"All my personal servants are women."

The center entrance opened into a long hall. Off the hall to the left was a Western-style living room complete with overstuffed furniture. The room to the right was Japanese style, the floor covered with straw matting. Three more girls waited just inside the door, all dressed in different costumes. From left to right, the first one was squeezed into a cashmere one-piece, curve-teasing outfit straight out of Bloomingdale's. The second wore the traditional Korean dress. The third girl was in a Japanese kimono, a fancy multicolored job held together by a wide golden sash. The gold obi was fighting a losing battle trying to hold down a bust that was far from Japanese.

Bonner barked rapid-fire orders at the women in Korean. Each of them took off in a different direction.

"They'll bring us food and drink. This way. I want you to meet my wife."

Carter couldn't suppress his surprise, and Bonner caught it.

"Oh, yes, I have a wife . . . and a harem. Tuan Lee is a very understanding woman, as are most Orientals."

By the time they got to a cozy sitting room with huge cushions on the floor around a low, round table, drinks and plates of food had preceded them.

Bonner settled in and pulled the tray of bottles toward him. "What would you like?"

"Scotch, neat," Carter replied.

He poured. "Just what do you do in the States, Mr. Crider? I mean, to be able to get your hands on all this sensitive gear?"

Carter accepted the glass and rattled off the cover story prepared for him by Pak and Kim Li. When he finished, Bonner seemed satisfied.

"Besides access, Crider, could you come up with contacts for shipping out of the U.S.? By that I mean—"

He stopped dead in mid-sentence. He was sitting facing the door. Carter's back was to it and he turned to see what had cut Bonner off.

The moment he saw her, Carter remembered walking along a lane in England years before with an old Scot. They had met a woman coming out of the fog and the old Scot had stopped with a gasp. He didn't speak until the woman was past and lost again in the fog.

"Aye, there's a woman that would put a thunderstorm in the blood," he had whispered. "She's lips that cling to the eyes and are as moist as a rose on a dewy morning. In my day, a woman like that would'a gone through the regiment like a forest fire. She's enough to make old Casanova rise in his grave! By God, if the old leg still had a little life, I'd be down the road after her a'ready. Take 'er from me own brother, I would. And did ya see the top? Most of 'em built like a board now, coffin chested. Not that one . . ."

He had gone on and on, and Carter had found it amusing.

Now he felt the same emotions.

She defied description. Standing quietly in the doorway, her strange beauty dominated the room so completely that for the moment everything else seemed unreal. She appeared to be Korean, possessing the high cheekbones and the pronounced Mongolian fold over her eyes, but a touch of Eurasian heightened her impossible beauty.

She wore a black skirt that almost hid her ankles and a white shirt; her middle was cinched in tight by a black belt with a simple brass buckle. She had a figure to rival Venus herself, and lustrous black hair that was rolled back into a wrapped chignon, so that it remained above the collar line. Her neck was long and free of lines, her skin pallid.

But it was her eyes that held Carter's attention. They were jet black and large, and seemed to have no bottom.

"Crider, my wife, Tuan Lee," Bonner said, and introduced her to Carter in Korean.

*"Annyong-hashimnika."*

She bowed slightly and smiled. That is, her sensual lips smiled, but not her eyes. The irises of those strange eyes should have been brown, or perhaps even dark gray or green . . . but not black. Carter couldn't distinguish the irises from the pupils. They caught his eyes and held them. The experience was similar to that of looking into the depths of a deep well, or into the total blackness of a bottomless abyss.

"Mr. Bonner is a very lucky man," Carter said.

Bonner interpreted and turned to Carter. "I'm afraid she only speaks Korean. You speak no Korean?"

"Very little," Carter said.

"It's all right," Bonner said, and shrugged. "She is a very dutiful Asian wife. She sits, eats, drinks, and nods while we talk. Sit. Back to business."

She spoke and Bonner interpreted. "Please do not let me disturb you."

The three of them sat, Tuan Lee slightly to the side, and fell to eating.

"What does she think of your harem?" Carter ventured.

"Nothing. She is an Oriental wife. She keeps her mouth shut and does what she's told."

That might be true, Carter thought, but he had the distinct feeling that Bonner had come right up on his toes when she'd entered the room. Also, if Bonner were so much the master, why did Carter get the feeling that right now the renegade Canadian was walking on glass?

As Carter enjoyed the food he darted quick glances at the woman out of the corner of his eyes.

Jacques Bonner's wife?

It was hard to believe. The idea that such an absolutely beautiful woman, with obvious grace and education, would marry someone like Bonner stretched the imagination.

Bonner was speaking again. "Now, what was I saying? Ah, yes, just what kind of contacts did you say you had in the States to acquire these components?"

"I just told you that," Carter said.

Bonner shrugged it off. "I know, but I like to make sure I have everything straight."

With a heavy sigh, Carter went through the whole thing again. And, as he spoke, he got the distinct impression that he was telling it all as much for the wife's edification as he was for Bonner's.

Finally the meal was consumed and one of the servant girls padded in to pick up the dishes. Another brought rice wine.

In the lull, Carter continued to examine the room. Everything was expensive, some of it slightly bizarre. Several of the works of art were pornographic. But it was expensive pornography, old Japanese prints by the masters that couldn't be found in art books.

There were also some oils, Japanese and Korean rural scenes, also several portraits. One full-length portrait of a young girl especially captured Carter's attention. As Bonner continued to question his ability to satisfy the illegal market for American and Japanese electronics, the Killmaster stood and paced to "stretch" his legs.

The closer Carter got to the portrait, the more familiar it seemed. It was of a young Korean girl of about twelve, perhaps thirteen, with long black hair framing an angelic face.

Bonner's wife?

Yes, he decided, the resemblance was striking, yet there were certain aspects to the face and body of the girl that didn't fit the mature woman daintily sipping rice wine.

Bonner caught Carter's interest. "That's one of my wife's favorites. She has amassed quite a good collection of oils, don't you think?"

"Indeed," Carter said, "quite a collection. Between the house and all this, I'd say you're not only doing well but you know how to invest for a rainy day."

Carter instantly saw that he had hit on Bonner's weak point, perhaps his only one: his own ego. The man instantly launched into a commentary on his major accomplishments since arriving in Korea.

Carter let him talk, encouraging him with a nod now and then and a smile.

Out of the corner of his eye, Carter watched Tuan Lee. She was throwing her husband a look so hard that the very air in the room seemed to turn black. Bonner was too wound up in his own conversation to notice.

Before he dug a hole too deep to get out of, she stood and, in rapid-fire Korean, suggested that it was late and perhaps it would be better for the two men to continue their business discussion in the morning.

Carter could catch enough of her little speech to get the gist, but he listened attentively to Bonner's translation as well as the man's reaction.

It was hard to imagine Jacques Bonner, with all his bravado and innate machismo, bowing to the smallest of a woman's suggestions, but this was obviously the case.

The Killmaster learned another interesting fact by the byplay: Tuan Lee understood English perfectly.

Suddenly the girl in the kimono appeared in the room. She stood demurely, her eyes to the floor, as if waiting for orders.

"She'll show you to your room, Crider," Bonner said, "and take care of all your needs." Then he chuckled and pushed the girl toward Carter. "Actually, it's a little ironic."

"How so?" Carter asked.

"This all started with you looking for Tomiko Mochiko. Well, there she is."

"Do you wish to make sex now or would you like a bath first?"

She was already half out of her kimono. Carter hadn't said two words to her, but she wasn't wasting any time doing exactly what Bonner had obviously told her to do.

Carter didn't answer her. He was too busy trying to put all the pieces together. Also, the portrait of the young girl was haunting his thoughts.

"I'm sorry that you don't find me attractive."

She was completely nude now and standing with her hands clasped tightly together over the dark triangle between her thighs. She was trembling.

"You are very attractive. How long did you know Toby Sukimoto?"

That caught her off guard but she recovered quickly. "Not long. Would you like some wine?"

Before Carter could reply she grabbed the bottle and began to pour clear wine into a small glass. But she was trembling more now, and suddenly she lost control completely. Her hands began to shake violently. The glass fell to the floor.

When she looked at Carter again her face was twisted with fear. He stepped toward her, thinking to pick up the glass. She backed away from him as if he were poison. As she did, she stepped directly into the illumination from the bedside lamp.

It was then that Carter saw the bruises on her body, and it all started to make sense.

"Did Bonner do that?" he murmured.

She paused, studying him as if she were trying to make up her mind about something. She sat on the bed and Carter searched the room. When he found a robe, he slipped it over her shoulders. She made no effort to pull it over her full, trembling breasts.

"Tomiko, I'm not going to beat you," he said softly, sitting beside her and taking one of her hands in his. "And you don't have to sleep with me."

Her head nodded violently. "Yes, I do. They would beat me if I didn't."

"They?"

"Bonner or Tuan Lee."

"*She* beats you?"

"*Hai*," she replied, not hiding the disgust in her voice. "She is worse than him. She is . . ." She glanced furtively around the room. Suddenly she got up and tiptoed across to the door. She stood listening for a moment, then quietly bolted the door from the inside. She tiptoed back and sat down beside Carter again. There were tears in her eyes and she was trembling uncontrollably. She was very feminine and looked more like a beautiful child than a mature woman. "You know Toby Sukimoto?"

"Yes," Carter lied.

"Where is he now? They won't tell me."

He squeezed her hand harder. "He's dead, Tomiko."

There were no sobs, but the tears squeezing from her swollen eyes increased.

"It is my fault," she choked. "They killed him because I betrayed him."

"Did you love him?"

"No, but he was a a nice boy and I betrayed him."

"How?" Carter said, placing a finger under her chin and turning her face to his.

For an instant the fear rekindled in her eyes, and then faded. She reached over and cupped his face gently between her hands and peered intently into his eyes.

"I think you are a nice man. Why do you do business with them?"

At this point it was a loaded question. Carter didn't want to blow his cover, but at the same time he wanted to gain her confidence.

"Nice men have to make money like everyone else, Tomiko. Just because I deal with Bonner doesn't make me like him or be like him." He waited for her to digest this before he spoke again. "Tell me why you think you were responsible for Toby's death."

She spoke haltingly at first, then, slowly, the words came rolling out. She had been a bar girl, by her own description nothing but a whore when she met Bonner in Seoul. He paid her huge amounts of money to sleep with him and do little errands.

This went on for almost a year. Then he brought her to Pusan and made her the head hostess at the Empire Casino. Not long after that, he bought her a huge wardrobe and sent her to Japan. Her instructions were to meet and seduce Toby Sukimoto at a party.

She was successful, so successful that the young Japanese took her back to the States with him as his mistress.

For eight months she kept Bonner informed of every move Sukimoto made, how he thought, right up until the time of his father's death.

"Then, right after I told them that Toby was meeting an American agent named Carter in Hong Kong, they ordered me back here. Since then I have been a prisoner, a chattel, in this house, little more than a slave to them."

"Tomiko, you keep saying *them*."

"That is because she, Tuan Lee, is even more evil than Bonner. She—"

Suddenly she stopped, her eyes wide. Then Carter heard it too, a slight footfall outside the door.

Tomiko took Carter's hand between both of hers and held it to her face and then to her breast. She leaned forward and brushed her lips over his.

"Ooohhh, so good, that feels so good. Why do you wait? Why don't you remove your clothes? Hurry, you will make me so happy tonight!"

Carter twisted around to face her and caressed her cheek. She closed her eyes and he kissed her. At first she only allowed it; then she threw her arms around him and kissed him with a devouring passion. She broke loose after a moment, seemed about to get off the bed, then grabbed him again and leaned him as far back as she could. She crawled up the length of him until she found his lips again. They lay like that for minutes, wordless, only kissing and breaking for a breath now and then for a few seconds. Her face was like fire to his touch, and she dug her fingernails into the back of his neck if he attempted to move away from her lips.

"Hurry!" she said aloud. "I can wait no longer. Remove your clothes!"

Carter slipped from the bed. As he removed his clothes, she lay naked watching him.

Both of them heard the padding footsteps retreat from the door.

As he turned the light off and slipped into the bed, Tomiko turned her back and buried her face in the pillow.

"Whoever it was is gone," Carter whispered.

"I know."

"Tomiko?"

"Yes?"

"There is another man, a boss over Bonner." He could feel her slender body tense beside him. "Do you know the name Dr. Kwon?"

Her head nodded. "Few people in Korea do not know the name of Dr. Kwon."

"Tomiko, have you ever seen Dr. Kwon?"

The silence went on for a long minute, then she turned to face him. "Once, when I first came here. He picked up Bonner at the casino in the big car..."

"The Mercedes?"

"Yes. They were to go to a very important meeting somewhere to the north."

"Did you see Kwon's face?"

"No. I only saw him in the back of the car from the shoulders down. His face was in shadows."

Carter digested this, tried again to piece it all together, and finally gave up, choosing sleep instead.

# FOURTEEN

Light fingered through the curtains. The window was partially open and a light breeze wafted into the room, bringing with it the scent of flowers and freshly brewed coffee.

Carter moved slightly within the cozy tent of the quilt. He slid his hand across the bed. The girl, Tomiko, was gone. Her scent still filled the room and the bed.

He slid a hand from beneath the snugness of the quilt and found cigarettes. He watched pale blue smoke climb in the room and let his mind go back to the problems and what he had learned thus far.

Who the hell was Dr. Kwon?

He had obviously terrorized a major portion of the population into fearing him. There was also respect there as well. He didn't hesitate to kill, but he used a foreigner to do it. Bonner was not unlike the Chinese hatchet men or the ancient Barbarian slave of Rome employed to torture prisoners in the games.

Could Jacques Bonner be Dr. Kwon?

Not according to what the girl, Tomiko, had told Carter.

She had seen Kwon in the back of the limousine.

Carter remembered the way Bonner had reacted to his wife. Could *she* be Kwon? It could perhaps fit. If the daughter of one of the men on Pak's list had all the information, it would be easy for her to use that information to put the organization back together. Then, to overcome the Oriental attitudes toward women, use Bonner to front the whole deal.

The aroma of the coffee drew Carter to the window. Bonner sat, reading and having breakfast, by one of the ornamental pools in the garden.

Carter showered, shaved, dressed, and joined him.

"Good morning. I trust you enjoyed the evening?"

"Immensely," Carter replied. "A very talented lady."

"Yes, I know."

One of the women appeared out of nowhere with a steaming plate of ham, eggs, and rice. She poured coffee and faded away.

As Carter attacked the dish, Bonner passed a sheet of computer paper over to him.

"That's a list of the items we could pass on for a tidy profit. How close do you think you could come to filling it?"

Carter made a great show of going over the lists. Most of the items he actually recognized.

"Sixty, perhaps eighty percent. Maybe more if the price were right."

"Excellent," Bonner said, and obviously meant it. "How soon do you think you could put an order of that size together?"

"That would take a few telephone calls to the States."

"Of course."

"I'll drive into Pusan later," Carter said.

"Of course," Bonner said with a tight smile, "from a

pay telephone. In the meantime, do you play tennis?"

"I have."

"Good." Bonner stood. "I'll have Tomiko lay out some things in your room. Meet you on the court. It's right over there beside the pool."

He left and Carter had a cigarette while he finished his coffee. He glanced up at the third-floor windows just in time to see Tuan Lee's face looking down at him before she dropped the curtain.

She was smiling, and for some odd reason it sent a chill up Carter's spine.

"Well, what shall we play for," Bonner asked, "just to make it interesting? Shall we say, what you contend I owe you?"

"I'm a gambler," Carter replied, "but I'm not a fool."

Bonner chuckled. "All right, just five thousand, then, best of three sets."

"Won?"

"Hardly, my friend. Dollars."

Bonner served, and Carter never saw the ball. The first game went 40-Love. Carter managed one point in the second game. Bonner won his serve again at 40-Love, and Carter bore down.

It did no good. Bonner won the first set six games to Love.

As they traded ends of the court, Carter murmured in passing, "Are you sure you were never on the tour?"

Bonner grinned. "Not at all. I just stay in shape."

Carter held his own to a three-three tie in the second set, and then Bonner turned loose with three straight games to win the match.

He even vaulted over the net to shake hands.

"You must work on your serve," he declared.

"And every stroke," Carter said dryly.

"Shall we say a bit of lunch and we'll drive into Pusan together?"

"I can drive myself," Carter said.

"Of course you can, but I'd like you to join me. I have a small chore to take care of this afternoon and you may enjoy it. Shower and change, I'll meet you in the gardens in an hour."

Carter made his way back to his room. Tomiko was there laying out a fresh change of clothes for him.

"You left before I could say good morning."

She bobbed her head and her body in the way Japanese women have, but didn't reply.

"Are you angry about something?"

"I have drawn bath."

She headed for the door and Carter caught her by the elbow. The moment he swung her around he saw it. The entire side of her face was turning an ugly purple and one eye was nearly swollen shut.

"Who did that?" he growled.

"Please . . ."

She struggled, but Carter held her tightly by both arms. *"Who?"*

"Tuan Lee."

"My God, why?"

"Because I found out nothing of value from you in bed last night."

"Damn," he hissed.

It was his fault. He knew why they had sent her to his bed. He should have remembered to give her something worthwhile to tell them instead of asking all the questions himself.

"I am sorry, Tomiko. I will be staying tonight and I will

make sure you have something to tell them in the morning."

It was painful but she managed a smile. "I told her nothing at all. I told her that you would not talk, that all you wanted to do was make love all night long."

Carter brushed the tip of her nose with his lips. "We just might manage that yet. I need another favor."

"I will try."

"Can you get your hands on a Polaroid camera?"

She thought for a moment, then nodded. "Yes, one of the other girls has one."

"Good. I want you to take a picture for me, a picture of the portrait in the small dining room. The one of the young Korean girl in the blue silk dress by the farmhouse. Can you do that?"

"I can do it. Is that all?"

"Yes. Oh, one other thing. Tuan Lee speaks English, doesn't she?"

"Oh, yes. She speaks many languages. I think maybe six or seven. She often speaks English with Bonner."

"I thought so. You go ahead."

She glided from the room and Carter headed for the shower, wondering what "little chore" Bonner had that he wanted Carter in on that afternoon.


"I can't help it! Kyo-shi, Orders are orders!"

Lee San Kyo hissed through his teeth and frowned at the instrument in his hand. "But what can I do about rioting students? That is up to the regular police and the militia."

"I know that, but if any ringleaders are picked up, it is up to you to interrogate them in case they have links to subversives, Communists. You know the routine."

Kyo rolled his eyes to the ceiling and cursed every ancestor of every one of his superiors in his mind.

"Kyo-shi, are you still there?"

"No. I am on my way to Yongdusan Park."

"I will file the report—"

Lee San Kyo punched a button and cut off the voice from K-CIA Central in Seoul. He punched another button and without waiting for a reply barked into the phone, "Have my car brought around to the side exit!"

He slammed the phone down and struggled into his coat. Halfway to the door, he remembered his gun and shoulder holster in the bottom drawer of his desk.

*The hell with it*, he thought, *one does not need a gun to interrogate snot-nosed, rock-throwing students.*

He descended to his car and cursed every student in Korea as he drove recklessly toward the core of the central city and Yongdusan Park.

The name meant Dragon Head Mountain, and it was symbolized by a large bronze dragon that stood at the edge of the grounds. The main feature in the park was Pusan Tower. It was 540 feet high, which commanded a magnificent view of the city below, the distant hills, and the entire sweep of the vast harbor and the sea.

Now, as Kyo nosed his car through the curious spectators, he could see that the dragon was almost obscured by tear-gas smoke, and clouds of it were rising toward the tower.

He was stopped at the barricades by a helmeted police officer, his Plexiglas face mask raised.

"I am sorry, but you can go no further."

Kyo flipped open his credentials case and held it before the officer's eyes. "What is the situation?"

"Not good, sir. They are throwing rocks and firebombs. Several cars have been turned over and burned."

"Any casualties?"

"Three so far," the officer said, and smiled. "All three were trampled by their own people."

Kyo nodded. He knew what that meant. The police had billy-whipped them to death and then pushed them under the feet of the retreating mob.

"What started this one?"

The officer shrugged. "Who knows how they start? One moment it's mothers with prams in the park, the next thing you know you have a thousand students and a riot."

Kyo sighed and got out of his car. "Any ringleaders caught yet?"

"Two. They are being held over there by the statue of Admiral Yi."

Kyo patted the officer on the arm and skirted the melee to head for the statue of Korea's most memorialized naval hero.

He never made it.

They picked him up simply and easily, scooping him out of the flowing crowd as an expert net caster traps a land-locked salmon. One of them grabbed his right arm. On the other side, a large man pressed the knife blade hard. Its sharp point slid through Kyo's jacket and put a cold kiss over his left kidney.

The prod moved him on, while a pair ahead dropped back to mask the scene.

When the knife eased, Kyo made his move, flinging back his head to crush a nose, sweeping his left fist around in a levered arc for the man holding his arm.

If the punch landed, Kyo didn't know it. Great and black, the weight pressed down on him, forcing him to his knees, smothering him in its choking folds. He remembered his cheek scraping the hardpack dirt, remembered a swaying, rocking-chair motion.

And then the blackness claimed him fully.

All the way in from the Tongnae district, Bonner made easy conversation about, of all things, Korean history. Carter found himself admiring the man's knowledge, if not the man himself.

"Of all the countries of the Orient, Korea, I think, has the most interesting and ironic background, from Don Gun to Syngman Rhee and beyond, to the fools in Seoul now."

"You do know your Korean history," Carter commented.

"I have the best of teachers . . . my lovely wife."

Carter darted a glance toward the front of the limousine where Tuan Lee sat silently by the driver. She had already been seated in the car when Carter got in, and her only answer to his greeting had been a curt nod.

"I know about all of them," Bonner continued, obviously enjoying his role as expert, "the Ee Dynasty, the Tonk, the Min . . . you can ask me anything about any of them."

"The Empress Min?" Carter asked.

"Ah, now there was a real woman. Married to a drooling idiot, she fought to be herself, to be a queen. And she was, despite the royal family, despite the Russians and the Japanese and yes, the Americans, too."

Bonner rattled on and on. Carter listened with half an ear, but he was impressed. He, too, knew the story well, but the way Bonner told it, Carter could almost see the former queen, the last empress of Korea, as she had been, an orphan girl, a commoner. Min Bi was intelligent, and shattered the Orient's taboo on women in government. She proved that a woman could be stubborn, too, that her vengeance was to be feared.

"She was hand-picked by Tae Wan Gun," Bonner said, "father of the emperor, when she was sixteen years old."

Carter nodded as Bonner continued, and suddenly he realized something in the telling. The speech was almost singsong as it came from Bonner's mouth, and it was too perfect.

It was as if he had learned every word by rote so he could repeat it without missing a fact.

The episodic tale was cut short as the car halted in the center of the Nampo-dong area. Bonner himself alighted from the car and opened the front door for his wife.

Tuan Lee stepped from the car, narrowing her square shoulders. Today she wore a blue pantsuit that made her seem thin, small-breasted, and almost boyish. Beneath the jacket, she wore a white blouse that came in ruffles clear to her neck. Low-heeled navy shoes and a large leather shoulder bag completed the ensemble.

As usual, the mane of glossy black hair was swept up and pulled back in a tight chignon.

She nodded once toward Carter in the back, and slid large sunglasses over her eyes as she turned to Bonner.

"How long will you be?" she asked in rapid Korean, not bothering to lower her voice since she was sure Carter spoke none of the language.

"Not much more than an hour, I think."

"I will need longer than that . . . perhaps two."

Bonner checked his watch. "I will bring him to the Commodore at five sharp."

"Good . . . and wait."

Throughout the entire exchange Carter kept his eyes on the passing parade in the street, smoking silently. He did not speak Korean, but he knew enough words to get the picture.

Again he was amazed at the way this woman spoke to Bonner. It was obvious that she was not under her husband's thumb.

Bonner slid back into the rear seat and rubbed his hands together.

"Now, we are both in for a rare treat!"

# FIFTEEN

The limo dropped into an underground garage. In the distance Carter could hear shouting and the unmistakable pop of tear-gas guns.

"What's going on?" he asked.

"Riot," Bonner replied, "in Yongdusan Park, just the other side of this building. Students, it happens all the time. Sometimes these little diversions are useful."

A steel door slid upward and the car moved into a huge storage room. When the door descended behind them, the sounds of the riot were gone.

Bonner and Carter got out of the limo. The chauffeur remained.

"This way."

Carter followed the white-suited man into a smaller room. There was a middle-aged Korean bound tightly to a straight-backed wooden chair. His coat and shirt were in tatters so that he was nearly naked from the waist up.

There were four goons standing in an arc around the rear of the chair. Each one of them looked capable of any type of mayhem.

As Bonner approached the bound man, he hissed loudly through his teeth and started to babble. "Bonner-shi, why do you do this? Why do you bring me here like this to lose face?"

Bonner backhanded the man across the face. "Silence! Kyo, you have no face. You are the son of a deceased whore!"

"Bonner-shi, I swear—"

Again the hand cracked across the man's face, and blood spurted from his crushed nose. Bonner quickly stepped aside so his immaculate suit wouldn't be sprayed.

"It was you, Lee San Kyo, who engineered the hijacking."

"No, no, I swear to you! It was I who told you where to find them, where to recover the shipment!"

"Yes, of course," Bonner said, "after you realized that you had no market for what you stole."

"Please, give me an audience with Kwon. He knows I would never betray him. Too many years I have served—"

"You have served yourself, Kyo. Seeing Kwon will do you no good. Ho Shan!"

From out of the shadows at the far end of the room, another man appeared. He was short and powerfully built. There was a thick bandage around his head, and ropes of muscle rippled under a tight black shirt.

In his right hand he carried a short, wooden club, similar to a policeman's nightstick. From the way it was balanced, Carter guessed it was heavily weighted with lead in one end.

"No, Bonner-shi, please, I beg of you . . ."

"Ho Shan!" Bonner barked.

The club whistled, twice, and there was no mistaking the sound of the man's right kneecap splintering.

Carter winced as a howl of agony erupted from the

man's lips and he writhed in pain against the ropes that held him. The Killmaster noticed that the ropes had been padded with cloth at the man's wrists and ankles so they would leave no burns on the skin.

"Bonner..."

"Yes?"

Carter stepped to the man's side. "What the hell did he do to deserve this?"

"He worked for us and betrayed us. That is all you need to know. Ho Shan!"

Again the club went to work, this time on the other kneecap. When it was no more than pulp, the powerful little Korean went to work on the ribs.

Carter's impulse was to stop it, but he knew if he did, the game was over. This was Dr. Kwon's form of justice, and the Killmaster knew that if he interfered, the image he had so carefully built up with Bonner as an equal would be shattered.

The man in the chair Bonner had called Kyo passed out.

Bonner snapped his fingers and the other four men went about reviving him.

"Retribution for misdeeds," Bonner said, "is very necessary to the continuation of fear. As I am sure you know, Crider, fear keeps men in their place. Shall we have some refreshment until the beginning of round two?"

The chauffeur had entered the room. He carried a tray. On it was a bottle of champagne and two properly chilled glasses.

Carter suppressed the bile that moved up toward his throat from his gut as Bonner calmly filled the glasses and handed one to him.

"When this pig is found, those in high places will know the truth. The men on the street will assume Kyo was killed by the mob. But our people will know. Your health."

Carter managed to sip from the glass. Now he knew the truth. This little exercise wasn't just a punishment. The man called Kyo was not going to leave this room alive. And Carter was powerless to stop it.

The screams of agony began again. Kyo was awake.

"Come," Bonner said, "let's enjoy the end."

Carter placed his glass on the tray and lit a cigarette to mask his mood. As they moved back toward the others, he saw a tiny bit of drool slide from the corner of Bonner's lips. His eyes were strained and they had turned red. Even his body was quivering with anticipation.

It was then that Carter realized Bonner's core. The man was in his element and he was insane: completely, totally insane.

"Cut the ropes and stand him up!"

This was done. Then Kyo was turned around, his arms stretched out by two men while two others held him by the ankles, spread-eagling his legs.

"Ho Shan," Bonner said, "the kidneys now. The coup de grace!"

The blows were sharp, precise, killing. It took only ten minutes for Kyo to die. When he did, the joy of it was over for Bonner. He became his old self at once.

"Shall we go?" he said calmly, turning to the door. "Where would you like me to drop you?"

Carter left the limo in the city hall area. He moved through shopping arcades and crisscrossed several streets until he spotted the tail Bonner had put on him. It took a little longer than usual because it was a woman instead of a man.

She was short, a little on the plump side, wearing a very touristy outfit of sunglasses, emerald green slacks, a gaudy shirt, and leather sandals. A camera hung around her neck and several recent purchases protruded from the shopping bag she carried.

He quickly found out that she wasn't very good at her job. She was too intent on her cover as the gawking tourist and kept stopping to buy little knickknacks. If Carter hadn't made it easy for her, she would have lost him a half-dozen times as he made his way to the international telephone exchange.

"I have several calls to the United States, and perhaps one or two inside Korea," he said to the operator.

"Of course, sir, booth three."

Through the international operator, Carter got his own number to his Georgetown condo and talked back to his answering machine for five minutes. The second number was off the top of his head, and so was the area code.

"Hello?"

"Yes, ma'am, to whom am I speaking?"

"Dinah."

"And where do you live, Dinah?"

"Houston, Texas. Who the hell is this?"

"This is the Round-the-World Fortune game, Dinah. What's your last name?"

"Oglethorpe. What did you say this was?"

"The Round-the-World Fortune game."

"Never heard of it," Dinah said, and hung up.

The third number was a little girl who couldn't call her mother to the phone because "Mommy's in the bedroom with my uncle and she can't be disturbed."

Carter managed to keep the little girl on the phone for nearly six minutes before she hung up on him.

*If Bonner has access to telephone company records,* Carter thought, *let him try to figure those out.*

The number in the house north of Seoul answered on the second ring. It was Kim Li's voice on a machine.

"You have reached 997-411," she said in Korean, and repeated it in English.

"This is Carter."

There was a click and her voice, without the metallic tone to it, came on at once. "Nick, how is it?"

"I'm in. In fact, I'm staying with Bonner and his wife."

"Where?"

"He has what amounts to a palace north of the city in Tongnae. They bought my story about ninety percent so far."

"They? You mean you've met Kwon? You know where he is?" There was practically breathless anticipation in her voice.

"Not so far, but I've got a hunch I'm getting close."

"How close?"

"Kim," Carter said, "what's the problem? I can hear something in your voice."

There was a few seconds' hesitation before she spoke again. "We have information that the North Koreans are planning to throw all their weight and all of the international distribution of the counterfeit money behind Dr. Kwon. There will be a meeting soon to solidify the agreement."

"How soon?"

"Two, maybe three days. Nick, we must put an end to Kwon before that meeting. We must, do you understand? We *must*."

"Hey, hey, take it easy. I'm working as fast as I can."

There was some heavy breathing on the other end of the line, but when she spoke again the control was back in her voice. "Of course you are right. I'm sorry. It's just that disrupting this meeting could be so important."

"I may have something," he replied. "I need you to dig into that master computer of Pak's in Hong Kong. I want you to go over all the the names on that probable list, and see if any of them had a daughter."

"A daughter? Buy why?"

"Did you ever stop to think," Carter said, "that Dr. Kwon could be a woman?"

"A woman? That's impossible!"

"Why?"

"Because," she sputtered, "it just is."

"Do it anyway. If there is a daughter, I want to know what she has been up to and where she is now."

"I think it's silly, but very well. Anything else?"

"Not right now."

"I'm coming down."

"What?"

"I'm coming to Pusan. If you uncover anything, I want to be right there. Two heads are better than one. You know how to reach me there. I should arrive early in the morning."

Before Carter could reply, she hung up. He did the same, and stood staring at the instrument for several seconds before going out to the desk and paying for the calls.

At the door he stopped at a bank of telephone books and thumbed through the Pusan directory until he found "Wo Fay Dak, Fine Art of Korea."

He checked his watch and hit the street. He still had nearly twenty minutes before the two hours that Tuan Lee had given Bonner were up.

Within a block of the telephone exchange, he spotted his young, female tail. He darted into the first bar he came to.

It was a dark, cool room that turned out to be a cabaret with a tiny L-shaped bar with eight stools, half a dozen tables crowded together, and a ten-foot-square dance floor with a raised dais that no doubt supported a band in the evenings. The only other occupant was a very bored-looking bartender who made a great show of polishing glasses when he saw Carter enter.

Carter climbed onto a stool and returned his greeting in his abortive Korean. All the bartender needed was to hear one word uttered in Carter's atrocious accent and he courteously lapsed into English which, although not good, was a hell of a lot better than Carter's Korean.

Carter automatically took a stool where he could watch the door in the mirror, and ordered a whiskey and soda. He guessed his tail didn't want to appear overanxious, so she gave him a full two minutes before she burst in the door and mounted a stool at the far end of the bar, scattering packages almost as far as the eye could see.

Carter had seen some amateurs in his time, but this one was something else. In order to impress him with the fact that she had wandered in there after him by a lucky coincidence, hadn't seen him, and wouldn't have recognized him anyway, she greeted the bartender as if she had been coming into the place her whole life.

Carter gave her a smile that forced a return. He picked up his glass and moved to the stool beside hers.

"Hello. Do you speak English?"

"A-A little," she said, nodding, clutching her glass of white wine with both hands.

"Can I buy you a drink?"

"No, thank you."

"I saw you looking at me. I figure that you're a working girl."

"What . . . ?"

"You're very cute. How about a hundred dollars? We can get a room . . ."

Her head tried to crawl into her shoulders. "Please, go away . . ."

"Look, bitch," Carter said, raising his voice to a shout, "what the hell is this?"

The bartender was right there. "Something is wrong?"

"You're damn right something is wrong!" Carter bellowed. "What kind of a joint is this? I give her money to go to a hotel with me and she says she changed her mind!"

The bartender snatched the glass of wine from her hands and in no uncertain terms told her to go back to Texas Town where she belonged.

She argued, but she was a woman. The bartender was a man and it was Korea. It was no contest.

Red-faced, she quit the bar. Carter saw her take up a new position in the window of a tea room across the street.

He ordered another drink and dropped a twenty on the bar.

When he had first come in he had spotted the men's room shielded by an alcove in the far rear of the bar. He had also spotted another door at the end of the hallway. He hoped it was the storage room.

It was, with a second door that led into an alley for deliveries.

Two streets away, he hailed a taxi.

"Commodore Dynasty Hotel, but not the front entrance. I'll show you where to park."

Carter had the taxi driver park about half a block from the side entrance to the hotel, telling him he wanted to wait for someone. The driver nodded and sat with his back to Carter and lit a foul-smelling cigarette, and they both listened to the steady clicks of the taxi meter reminding them that nothing in Korea is free.

Carter slouched in a shadowy corner of the cab and kept an eye on the doorway. Once, the driver turned around to look at Carter. His face was a blob of flesh with two tiny black eyes beneath a wrinkled forehead. He opened his mouth in a smirky smile and showed half a dozen stained teeth.

"A woman?" he said.

"Yes," Carter replied.

The man giggled and sucked on the cigarette again before throwing it out his open window.

Five minutes later, the limousine pulled up to the curb. Bonner jumped out and held the door. At the same time, the glass door of the hotel opened and a young man wearing a modish, dark suit, a dark tie, and wrap-around sunglasses emerged.

He was maybe thirty. His hair was long over his collar, nearly covering the top half of his ears. His soft, black leather shoes glistened as he walked with a springy, athletic stride and darted into the black limousine.

"Two hundred American dollars," Carter said, "if you can follow that car without being spotted."

"Oh, yeah. Hokay, let's go!"

The ride was about twenty minutes, out to Chosan Beach. The driver stopped about three blocks away from the alley where the limo had disappeared.

"Hokay?"

"Great. Wait," Carter said, and bolted from the cab.

It was an area of new, high-rise luxury condominiums, all facing the ocean and jammed together around their own courtyards.

Carter hit the mouth of the alley and saw that it ran down into an underground garage. He trotted to the ramp and darted behind a pillar where he could see the parking area and the courtyard.

Bonner and the younger man were just crossing the courtyard. They entered the elevators, and Carter watched the digital dial go to ten and stop.

He checked the names of the apartments and the address, and returned to the cab.

"Okay," he said to the driver, "can you find this place?" He gave him the address of the gallery.

"Ah, yes, no sweat."

It was dusk when Carter arrived at the gallery, just as the neon was going on along the narrow streets. Carter got out and paid the driver. The street was crowded with milling people. Korean and tourists alike. Spoken Korean was discordant in his ears, combined with the minor-key Oriental music emanating from a nearby shop. There was the odor of a wood fire from somewhere, and of exotic foods cooking.

Carter opened the glass door to the gallery, entered, and closed it behind him. It was as if an electronic control had turned the sound down to a whisper when the door closed. The outside world had disappeared.

Prints and original oils crowded every inch of wall space. In glass cases he saw pen-and-ink drawings on parchment that looked to be hundreds of years old.

"Good evening, may I help you?"

Carter turned just as the heavily embroidered curtain fell behind her. She was tall for a Korean, and slim with a feminine slenderness that accented the swells of her figure in the traditional Korean costume.

"I certainly hope so. My name is Nick Crider. I'm a writer and an amateur art historian."

"I am Toi Khai. How can I help you?"

Carter took from his pocket a scrap of paper. On it he had carefully traced the signature of the artist from the painting of the young girl.

She studied it for several moments, and then her face lit up with a smile. "I am sorry to take so long. It is the signature of Sing Hee Youl. He has painted many portraits. His portrait of your General MacArthur hangs in our national gallery."

"There is a certain picture I would like to purchase. I wonder if you would have a catalogue of Youl's work?"

"Oh, yes. Come this way, please."

Carter followed her through the brocade curtain and waited while she went through her files. At last she dropped a book nearly a foot thick in front of him. "Sing Hee Youl was very prolific."

"I can see that," Carter said with a sigh.

She laughed. "Don't worry. We do not close until ten. Would you like some tea?"

"I would love some tea."

It took Carter nearly two hours to go through the book. When he finally turned the last page, it was with a sigh of disgust.

There wasn't a painting in it that even came close to matching the one on Bonner's wall.

The girl lifted her eyes from the papers on her desk. "No luck?"

"I'm afraid not. Are you sure all of his work is represented here?"

She came around the desk and flipped the book open to the frontispiece page. Her eyes darted from side to side over the print and turned to Carter.

"There were some privately commissioned portraits that were never offered for public sale. Not many, but since there is no record of them, they are not in the book."

"Damn," he growled, and rubbed his temples. "I don't suppose there is any way of locating Sing Hee Youl, is there?"

"Oh, I don't know. If he is still alive he would be a very, very old man now."

"Well," Carter sighed, getting to his feet, "I guess that's it."

"Wait. There is a chance. My art history professor at the university would know."

Carter smiled at her. "It's worth the most expensive dinner in Pusan."

She blushed and reached for the phone.

Five minutes later, Toi Khai had enough dollars for a holiday weekend, and Carter had the location of Sing Hee Youl's studio in Talsong Park near Taegu.

He whistled all the way to the casino to catch his ride back with Bonner in the limo.

# SIXTEEN

Her eyes popped open the moment Carter's body moved beneath the quilt. She smiled and took his hand between both of hers and drew it to the valley between her breasts. She held it there and moved into him until he could see only the top of her head.

Carter had no fear now of Tomiko Mochiko. Quite the opposite. Without really knowing what she was getting into, she had willingly become his fellow conspirator. He had no illusions. He knew it was her fear and loathing of Jacques Bonner and Tuan Lee—as well as her guilt about the fate of Toby Sukimoto—that prompted her.

But that, and the confidence he seemed to have built in her toward him, would make her a faithful friend for the duration.

The previous night's ride back from Pusan had been strange. Both Bonner and Tuan Lee seemed to be in high spirits. Bonner had even mentioned the girl he had assigned to tail Carter.

"The poor thing was petrified that you had given her the slip so easily."

"You shouldn't use amateurs," Carter had replied.

"It isn't important," Bonner had said with a shrug. "She was to watch for anyone else watching you. That job she did."

Carter had almost believed him.

He had barely reached his bed when Tomiko had come into the room and slipped into the bed beside him. There was no holding back this night. Without words they had come together. She was all thrusting hips and mewling cries of desire. Her body was magic and brightness run mad in the darkened room.

"You think very hard," she said, her voice muffled against his chest.

"How can you tell that?"

"Your heart. It follows the dictates of your brain. It beats very fast, then slows, and fast again as you think."

*Oh*, he thought, *the mysteries of the East*.

Her hair was very black and slightly disarranged. He turned his face and touched his lips lightly to the top of her head. She pressed his hand harder between her breasts; his hand was warm, but her body was warmer. She snuggled closer to him. He stroked the smooth shape of her bare back.

"Tomiko, have you ever been on the third floor, in Tuan Lee's rooms?"

"Oh, no never," she exclaimed with a shake of her head. "No one is allowed on the third floor!"

"What about maids, cleaning?" he asked.

"No one, never."

Carter digested this before he spoke again. "Tell the cook to fix a lunch. We're going on a picnic today."

"A what?"

"A basket of food. We are going to a park and eat under the trees." He rose from the bed.

"Now?"

"Now."

She giggled. "A bath and breakfast first."

He soaked in the near-scalding water with her, sipping unsugared green tea while the heat reached the marrow of his bones.

Then, outside on the patio, he ate, eggs and steak, thick slabs of toast golden with butter, coffee, all of it excellent.

He was on his second cup of coffee and a cigarette when Jacques Bonner emerged from the house headed for the limousine. He paused at Carter's table.

"We'll be gone most of the day, Crider. Do you think you'll have word from your contacts by this evening? I would like to be able to tell my buyers in a day or so that we can deliver."

Carter nodded. "I don't think there will be any problem."

Bonner smiled and dropped his hand on Carter's shoulder. "Good, good. I like you, Crider. I think we're going to have a very profitable relationship."

He moved off and Carter stopped him with his voice. "If the tail you put on me today loses me, tell him to head for Taegu. I'm going picnicking with Tomiko."

"Oh, I don't think there's a need for that anymore," Bonner replied. "Have a good time."

*Oh, I think I will*, Carter thought. *Before the day is out, I think I will have an extremely good time!*

Carter cruised through the city of Taegu following Tomiko's directions as she read the Korean road signs. It was a lazy day, the kind to which people look forward during the stormy days of February and March. The sky was deep and still. The only movement was an occasional jet leaving a thin vapor trail like the stroke of an artist's brush or a stray cloud that now and then sailed past in the form of a puffy white spinnaker. It was the kind of day for one to relax and think pleasant things.

Carter almost wished that a picnic really was the reason for the drive.

"There, that is the lane," Tomiko said, checking the notes she had made when she had asked directions of the gate guard when they entered the park.

Carter wheeled the car into a tiny dirt road almost hidden by trees and bushes. They drove a tortured mile along the rough surface through a range of low wooded hills.

"We must stop here," she said, "and walk the rest of the way."

It was an idyllic setting, a hidden haven of grass-covered low hills, shady trees, picnic shelters, and small hibachis for the charcoal cooking of food. And near the road, dug into the side of a tree-covered hill, was a small lake fed from a clear stream of water that flowed into the side of the pool from other hills to the north. It had been constructed laboriously of large flat rocks. On the deep and against the hill, the rock construction continued as a series of stone steps or benches for observers or divers.

It was a wonderful spot for a picnic, for an outing, for swimming and Tomiko in a tight bikini, for Korean beer and good things to eat.

Only they had other things to do.

The park was deserted now. Carter helped Tomiko from the car and looked around. As far as he could see, the tiny road was the only entrance. It ended in a large grassy area between two hills. They were surrounded by the hills on three sides and by heavy junglelike foliage on the other. If anyone came in by the road, they would spot him.

Carter locked the car and they set off through the trees on a path that led around the lake. On the far side they came into a clearing, and there was the studio of Sing Hee Youl.

It was little more than an A-frame hut with bamboo panels in the roof that could be pulled aside to let in the sun. A small lean-to on the side looked to be sleeping quarters.

As they crossed the packed earth toward the lean-to, they could smell food cooking and see smoke slithering through the cracks near the roof.

The door was wide open, and an ancient man squatted before a charcoal burner stirring food in a pot.

"*Yoboseyo*," he said without turning.

Carter poked Tomiko in the ribs and she took off in Korean. He hoped she was giving the old man the cover story they had gone over during the drive.

She was just winding down when the old man turned to face them. The little man was gnarled, his face layered by wrinkles, his eyes twinkling.

There was the rapid hiss of indrawn breath, the signal of surprise, and then he spoke, perfect English, in a low, modulated voice.

"It has been many years since anyone has been interested in the work of Sing Hee Youl. Come in, my children, we will eat and then we will talk of art."

He straightened as much as his bent back would allow, and motioned them to pillows at the low dining table. He found wine, glasses, and two extra plates.

"We will have *kimchi*, a little *soju*, if it please you."

"We would be honored," Carter said.

Sitting cross-legged on the floor, they ate the pickled cabbage and white radishes spiced with garlic and green onions and laced heavily with powerful dried peppers.

Carter could feel his face burning and tried to keep the fire under control with glass after glass of rice wine.

"The *kimchi* is strong," the old man cackled. "I do everything the old way, even make my *kimchi* strong enough to boil the stomach of a dead man. Eat, my American friend. It will always remind you of Korea, this *kimchi*!"

"I can believe it," Carter croaked, and forced another spoonful into his mouth.

"I am ninety-one and I have never been to a medical man in my life. I treat myself with Tiger Balm, ginseng, cobwebs ground to a fine powder, oils from the great shark . . ." He paused and eyed Carter. "You do not laugh at an old man who clings to the things of his youth?"

"No," Carter said, meeting the other's steady gaze. "All things new come from the old. Sometimes the old things are best."

"*Chong-mal*, in truth. Now, why have you come to see me?"

Carter passed him the Polaroid photo of the painting. Youl studied it for several minutes, and then rolled his bright eyes toward Carter.

"It is one of two."

"What?"

"I remember that there were two children, a few years apart in age. I painted both of them for a very powerful man. He paid me for both, but took only one of the paintings, the girl. The painting of the boy child he had me destroy."

"And did you destroy it?" Carter asked.

A shrug. "It was his money."

Something tickled Carter's brain into asking the next questions. "For an oil such as this, you would have made sketches first. I would like to buy those sketches."

The old man nodded. "I may have them."

"And names," Carter added. "I would like the names of the family."

Sing Hee Youl hesitated for a moment and then climbed achingly to his feet. "Follow me, please."

They followed him into the studio where for the next hour he rummaged through makeshift bins. At last he found the sketches and spread them out before Carter.

One by one, the Killmaster went through them. And with each one, the picture became clearer. He saw the sketches build into the two portraits of the girl and the boy.

"The names? Do you have the names?"

It took another hour of poking through musty files, but Youl found them at last.

Carter paid him far more than the sketches were worth, and rolled them carefully under his arm. Then, thanking the old man profusely for his hospitality, they took their leave.

"You found what you were looking for?" Tomiko asked as they walked back to the car.

"More than I was looking for," Carter replied.

"What do we do now?"

"We go to Pusan and become burglars."

A few blocks from the Commodore Dynasty, Carter stopped at a department store and bought two suitcases. In a used-book store he purchased two stacks of books that would add weight to the luggage.

At the hotel, he passed the bags to a porter and entered the lobby with Tomiko on his arm.

"Just one night. I'm sorry I don't have a reservation. Would you have a suite available?"

A check was made and there was a suite available with two bedrooms. Carter registered under his Crider passport, and put Tomiko down as his interpreter and secretary.

The clerk smirked but said nothing.

"I'm liable to be in Pusan for an extended period of time," Carter said. "Do you have term leases on the suites?"

"Yes, sir, we do. Several companies have arrangements with us."

"Good, good. Is there any kind of choice, as far as floors are concerned?"

"There are only eight suites, sir, two each on the top four floors."

"And are all of those available?"

"There are five available, sir."

"I see. Excellent, thank you."

In the elevator with the porter and the bags, Carter did mental calculations. There were fourteen floors. That meant the suites were distributed between floors eleven and fourteen. Three of the eight were leased.

The elevator stopped at fourteen and the porter led them to the very end of the hall.

"The other suite on this floor," Carter said, "is it on a long lease?"

"No, sir, not rented now."

*So much for fourteen*, Carter thought.

"And where would it be, in relation to this one?"

The question was a little too much for the porter's English. Tomiko translated. The other suite was a mirror image of the one they now entered, and it was located at the far opposite end of the hotel.

Carter was tempted to pump the man a little further and sweeten it with a big tip, but he didn't. Bonner and Tuan Lee most likely passed their own tip around the hotel staff. Anyone asking too many questions would be suspect and the word would get back to one or both of them.

As soon as the bellman was gone, Carter explained the procedure to Tomiko.

The hotel was large and well staffed. He expected that there would be four maids, two carts, to a floor. If they followed the same procedure that nearly every hotel in the world followed, the bulk of the cleaning would come between ten in the morning and two in the afternoon, two hours each side of the noon check-out time.

It was now twelve-thirty and the maids were probably harassed.

"Wait," Carter said, and slipped from the room.

It was easy: just follow the sound of a television set to an open door. Just inside the door was the maid's cart. A clipboard hung on one end of it with the day's cleaning log for that floor.

The maid was cleaning the bath. Carter flipped the pages to a blank log sheet and tore one out.

Back in the suite, he went over it with Tomiko. She explained the Korean symbols to him, and he told her what to look for in the space for penciled notations.

Together they headed for the eleventh floor.

It turned out to be simple. All four of the maids were working out of one cart. The other cart was parked by the elevators.

Tomiko scanned the current day's chart and the duplicates for the past days of the week. When she nodded, they moved on up to twelve. This time Carter had to act like a beleaguered guest with one of the maids to shield Tomiko as she went through the log.

There was no need to check thirteen. The doors to both suites were open and the maids were inside, cleaning.

"Why is there no need to check?" Tomiko asked.

"Because, if Tuan Lee won't let the maids into her third-floor apartments at the house to clean, I'm guessing it's the same with the suite here at the hotel."

Back in their own suite, they consulted Tomiko's hurriedly written notes.

All the suites were named, rather than numbered, after constellations. Their suite was Orion. The two on the twelfth floor were Ursa Major and Ursa Minor.

In the column for Ursa Minor for every day there was a "Do not clean" notation.

In the same column for every other suite, there was a "Clean" notation for at least two days of the week.

Tomiko smiled. "Ursa Minor never gets cleaned."

"That's right."

"What do we do now?"

"We relax until a little after two. The rush will be over, and that's when the maids will probably take their lunch break."

Just to be safe, Carter rapped on the door of Ursa Minor. There was no reply from inside, and the corridor was empty.

He pulled his personal key ring from his pocket. On it were a number of picks. In knowledgeable hands one of the ten picks would open any lock made by man.

It took two minutes to find the right pick and open the door. He ushered Tomiko inside and closed the door behind them.

"Stay here and listen. Just in case," he instructed her.

The suite was identical to theirs . . . sitting room, bedroom, dressing area, and bath.

As Carter took it in, he noticed that even though it was leased on a long-term basis, it looked no more lived-in than their own Orion Suite.

He went to work. He started in the bathroom, checking the tank on the toilet, the shower curtains, underneath the sink, then the inside of the medicine cabinet. There was nothing. He moved to the other room.

He checked everything on and under the bed. He went over the curtains and looked under the carpeting. He even went over the balcony. He moved on to the drawers in the dresser, pulling it out to look at the back. Everyplace he searched, he made sure that he left no prints.

There was nothing left but a large, walk-in closet, and the moment he opened the door he knew he had struck pure gold.

There were two racks, all full of fine-quality, expensive clothes. The odd part was that all the clothes on the left were for a woman. All the clothes on the right were for a man. Below both racks were shoes, some for a man, some pair for a woman.

Jacques Bonner and Tuan Lee? he wondered.

Hardly.

Bonner's shoulders would split the men's jackets before he could get into them. And the shoes wouldn't accommodate his big toe.

On the shelf above the clothes, wrapped in plastic bags, were ten wigs on stands. All the wigs were expensive, human-hair models, and each of them had been coiffed in a different style.

Carefully, Carter closed the door just the way he had found it, and joined Tomiko.

"You find what you look for in there?"

"All of it," he said, nodding. "Let's go."

He deposited her back in the Orion Suite.

"I want you to stay here. If you need anything, get it from room service. Don't go out."

"I want to go with you . . ."

"No," Carter said firmly, "you stay here." He started for the door of the suite, then paused and turned back to her.

"And, Tomiko, you won't be going back to the house in Tongnae anymore."

He took the elevator down and hit the bank of pay phones beside the lounge.

The first two calls he made were to Washington. The third call was to the Pusan number that Kim Li had given him.

She answered immediately, and gave him the directions to Pak's safe house in the Haeundae Beach area.

# SEVENTEEN

The house was small, in a wooded, secluded area near the coast. The two shadows Carter remembered from the house up the coast came from out of the shrubbery, checked him out, and waved him through the gate.

Kim Li was waiting for him at the door in a red silk housecoat. It was loosely tied, and he could tell she wore nothing beneath it.

She said nothing as he stepped through the door. Instead, she glided into his arms and her mouth crushed his, opening, avid. The color of her skin was golden, but her lips were red, and her body was wild as it surged against him.

"Have you missed me so much?" he asked, finally pulling himself loose from her grip.

"Of course." Her eyes narrowed, studying his mood. "What is it? What's the matter?"

"It's been a rough couple of days. Let's have a drink."

"Of course."

She rushed to fix them, speaking over her shoulder as if

everything she said was a second thought. "You have found Kwon?"

"I think so."

"Who is it?" Her hand trembled as she handed him the glass.

"I think I can tell you by morning. In fact, I should know right after I get back to the house."

"Why not now?" Her voice was sharp, the tone demanding.

"Kim, if we are going to kill the man, I want to make sure we have the right one. Don't you agree?"

"Of course. I'm sorry. Now that we are so close, I am tense."

Carter weighed his next words carefully. "I've done a lot of digging, Kim."

"Oh?"

"Yes. I think there might be a way to dismantle Kwon's operation and make him run. That would be a lot better than killing him, don't you think?"

She took a long time to answer. "I don't know. I would have to talk to Pak San Roo. It would be his decision."

Carter finished his drink and stood. "No, it wouldn't."

"What?"

"It's mine, Kim. Since I am going to have to do the killing, it's *my* decision."

"I will speak to Pak," she said, moving in close. "Must you go now?"

He felt the thick feathers of her hair across his throat and the firmness of her breasts against his chest. Her lips moved against his ear, her whisper warm. "I have missed you, Nick."

"I'm afraid there is no time. I have to get back to Tongnae."

"Is Kwon in Bonner's house at Tongnae?"

"Not now," Carter lied, "but I think he may be before morning. By the way, the information I asked you to obtain, about the daughters?"

"Oh, yes." She slipped from his arms, crossed the room, and came back with a slip of paper. "There are three alive. None of them is in Korea. Why your interest in the daughters?"

"Because I'm almost sure that the reason you and Pak were never able to find Kwon is that you were looking for a man." He headed for the door and then paused. "Also, you mentioned a meeting . . ."

"Yes, between the North Koreans and Kwon. It is set for tomorrow night. Nick, that meeting must never take place!"

Carter smiled. "It won't."

He left the house and drove north on the coastal highway. At a gas station, he used the pay phone to call Washington and get the information updates requested in his earlier calls. He also gave them the instructions for what he would need in the next twenty-four hours.

Carter passed through the gates with a wave to the guards that wasn't returned. The limousine was not in its usual place. He bent low and looked up through the windshield to peer at the windows of the third-floor apartment.

They blazed with light.

The solitary guard who stayed inside the house at all times lingered by the stairs. Carter walked up to him.

"Bonner-shi?" he asked.

"Pusan. Back soon," the man replied flatly.

Carter hit him, center gut, with everything he had. The head snapped forward, the long black hair flopping over his eyes. Carter caught the cheek on a lifted knee and changed the head's direction.

He went over the falling man, chopping hard knuckles at his arm, at the glint of blue metal in his hand. The gun kicked away and clanged off the far wall. Carter curled a grip around the smooth wrist and jerked the man toward him, veeing a spread thumb and fingers into the exposed throat, slamming like the edge of a hatchet into the vulnerable larynx.

The gunman choked backward, flailing arms that had no strength to them, gagging, sucking for air that would not pass his ruptured throat. Carter gave him mercy: he put his weight into a pivoting hook that landed flush, and the man felt no more pain.

The Killmaster dragged him into a nearby closet and locked the door after him.

On the second floor he loudly entered his own rooms, slamming the door behind him. In the bath, he turned the shower on full blast. Returning to the hall door, he snapped on the television and let it blare.

Quietly, he let himself into the hall and climbed the stairs to the third floor. Gently he tried the knob. It was locked.

He backed off four paces and pulled the Luger from the shoulder rig. When his shoulder hit the door, the jamb splintered like tissue paper. The door flattened and Carter went right over it.

He was at the bar pouring a drink. The bottle crashed to the floor and the hand darted toward a drawer.

"Don't," Carter growled, lifting the Luger.

The hand stopped and calmly reached for a cigarette lighter. "May I?"

"Sure," Carter replied.

The cigarette was in an ivory holder. Elegantly, the perfectly manicured hands lifted the flame to the cigarette. He took a deep drag and leaned against the back bar counter.

He made an extraordinarily handsome figure, if somewhat pretty. The hair was neatly trimmed around small, almost dainty ears. A pair of striking, tar-black eyes peered from a face that, although delicate, seemed cast from a perfect mold.

A navy-blue blazer and light-blue denim slacks covered a frame that seemed to be that of a trim, average-size male. A shirt was open at the neck displaying a light-blue ascot.

But undoubtedly the smile was the most dazzling aspect of the appearance. It was relaxed and confident . . . a smile that only one who was the proprietor of such splendid features could deliver.

"You know, of course."

Carter nodded. "Since this morning. I became sure this afternoon."

"It would be interesting to know what made you suspect."

"The portrait, in the small dining room. The resemblance is fantastic."

A slight hiss of air and then a sigh as he moved with lithe confidence around the bar and sat on one of the stools. His movements were masculine, but had a certain feminine grace.

"Jacques often told me that keeping that portrait around was a mistake. I suppose it was a piece of silly sentiment. I am curious, though—how did it happen to make you suspect?"

"I thought it was you as a young girl at first. But when I saw Sing Hee Youl, I discovered the truth."

"Ah, yes, the artist. I didn't realize the old fool was still alive. Is your name really Crider?"

"No, Carter. I am the American agent that Toby Sukimoto contacted to meet him in Hong Kong."

The eyes narrowed and the bland calm left the face.

Carter could sense the evil that coursed through him, the lust for power that ripped with sharp nails and slashed with sharper teeth.

"You make a beautiful woman," he commented. "Without the portrait, and what I found out from the artist, I would never have guessed."

A hand brushed smoke from his eyes. "In school in Japan, as a boy, I studied Noh and other forms of Japanese drama. Because of my size I was always given the women's roles. You must agree, no one would think of looking for Dr. Kwon as a woman."

"No," Carter agreed, "particularly those who knew already that Dr. Kwon was a man. It was Pak and Kim Li who sent me to kill you."

The face became animated, first with glee and then surprise. "Really? How ingenious! And they know that you're an American agent?"

"Yes. They couldn't find you. They assumed a crooked Caucasian would."

A nod and a shrug. "A good plan. I would never have expected it. But do you know everything?"

"There are a few holes."

Carter went through what he suspected, and the other man blithely filled in what he didn't know.

"And so, what do you propose to do now? Kill me?"

"Not unless I have to. I want the names of everyone in the Dr. Kwon organization. The people who take the graft in the police, the militia, and the government. I want the names of your overseas contacts, the people who distribute the phony money."

"In other words, you want it all."

"That's it. Where you go, what you do, I don't give a damn. Without the names, there is no more Dr. Kwon anyway."

"Quite right. But I am afraid I will have to stop you. Tell him how, Jacques."

Carter half turned. Bonner stood in the doorway. The two shadows from the main gate were right behind him. Directly in front of him was Tomiko Mochiko, with the point of a very ugly knife at her belly.

"One of the maids saw you leave the hotel suite," Bonner said. "She is paid very well to inform us of such things. How much does he know?"

"He knows that I am Tong Li. He guessed most of the rest."

Carter had the Luger still leveled. "It's a stalemate, Bonner."

Bonner smiled. "I don't think so. I don't think you've got the guts. I'll carve out her whole middle."

"You're right," Carter said, and flipped the Luger around to hold it by the barrel.

All of them were very surprised that he had given up so easily.

The pain came the moment Carter opened his good eye. He could tell that the other one was swollen shut. His back and ribs were sore where they had kicked and beaten him. Other than that, he was whole and operable.

"You are awake?" It was Tomiko. Slowly she came into focus.

"Yeah, half."

"They beat you very badly."

Carter managed a smile through his cracked lips. "Believe me, it looks worse than it is."

"They will kill us now, won't they."

"No," he said, "not until they interrogate me more. They need to know how much I have told my government.

They won't kill us until they know that, and by then we'll be out of here."

"But how . . . ?"

"You'll see."

He groaned, managed to roll himself to a sitting position, and looked around. They were in a dirt-floored cell. It was about twelve by twelve, with plaster walls painted a sickly green. There were no windows.

"Where are we?"

"A room under the house," Tomiko replied. "It is some kind of a cellar."

He felt in his pockets. They had left him his cigarettes and lighter. He got one lit and let the smoke wake him up by burning his throat and lungs.

Tomiko sat beside him on the cot. "There is so much that I do not understand. Who is the man who called himself Tong Li? I have never seen him before."

"That, Tomiko, is the person you know as Tuan Lee."

"A man who is a woman?" she gasped.

"A man who hides as a woman so he cannot be found. He also wanted to be known as Dr. Kwon."

"You mean, that is Dr. Kwon?"

"No," Carter said, forcing himself to concentrate, "that is the man who would be Dr. Kwon."

"I don't understand."

Carter squeezed her hand. "It's better that you don't understand, Tomiko."

Suddenly, above them, all hell broke loose. The walls were thick enough to hold them in, but not thick enough to shut out completely the chatter of machine pistols. Soon the gunfire was accompanied by shouting and the screams of death.

"What is that?" Tomiko cried.

Calmly, Carter crushed out his cigarette. "Our rescue party."

The door to their cell opened twenty minutes later. Two men, all in black, brandishing Ingram machine pistols, burst into the room. One of them shined a flashlight on Carter's face.

"You are the American, Carter. Correct?"

"Correct."

"Come, hurry, this way!"

Carter moved through the door and up the stairs. Kim Li was at the top of the stairs. She, too, was all in black, with a ski mask over her face and carrying an Ingram.

"It's done?" Carter said.

She nodded. "You must get out of Korea at once. We all must."

"I'll drive to Seoul and get the morning plane."

"What about her?" Kim said, gesturing to Tomiko with the Ingram.

"She knows nothing, but she has helped me. I'll take care of her. I'll have to see, to make sure, so I can tell my people."

"Of course," Kim replied. "Put the girl in his car. This way!"

One of the black-clad men ushered Tomiko away. Carter followed Kim through the house. Each room they passed through was a shambles.

"I thought you would come," he said.

"I had to. You might not have been able to handle them all by yourself. Besides, you practically told me."

Carter only nodded. They stepped over two dead guards on the lower landing, and climbed the stairs. At the top, a third guard lay practically cut in half.

"This one lived long enough to tell us where you were being held."

Bonner was at the landing at the top of the third-floor stairs. A black-clad figure was sprawled across his legs, as if the two of them had embraced in death.

They must have put at least two full magazines into Bonner to kill him. His face was gone, along with most of his chest and one shoulder.

"How many did you lose?"

"Three," Kim replied. "That one, Bonner, was a devil. He wouldn't die." She said it without a quiver in her voice.

They moved on into the third-floor apartments. The living room was a shambles. Every inch of space had been searched. Furniture was ripped open, books were torn apart, even sections of the wall had been torn away.

"Did you find anything?"

"Some cash, papers, tapes." She nodded toward the fireplace, where what had been a good-sized fire not long before was now smoldering ashes.

"Did you have to do that?"

"It is better this way. Without the head the body will mold. I saved the last shipment of components. They are in the trunk of your car. You can give them back to your people."

Carter sighed wearily. "Where is he?"

"In the bedroom."

Carter crossed and entered the bedroom. Tuan Lee alias Tong Li, the man who would be Dr. Kwon, was lying facedown across a blood-smeared bed.

Carter rolled him over. The Killmaster's own Luger was in the man's hand. There was a neat hole in the right side of his temple. The left side of his head was spread across the headboard.

"He killed himself?"

"I gave him that choice when I came into the room."

She was looking toward the door, away from the body. Carter knew she hadn't touched it. He guessed she hadn't looked at it either.

"You can tell your government that the infamous Dr. Kwon is now dead for good."

"Yeah," Carter replied, slipping the Luger from the dead man's grip and sliding it into his shoulder rig, "I'll tell 'em that. You didn't burn the cash, did you?"

"What?"

Carter moved past her and went back into the living room. "The cash. You burned everything else. You said you found cash. Surely you didn't burn that?"

"No. It's there, in that briefcase by the door."

Carter upended the briefcase. There was a lot of won and a lot of yen and about twenty thousand in American dollars. All in all, it looked like about fifty thousand, without the won.

"I'm taking the yen and dollars."

"What?"

"I've got a good place for it. You don't need it."

She had a look of amazement on her face, but she didn't object as she followed him down to the second floor.

"What happened to the other girls?" he asked, going from room to room until he found Tomiko's.

"Dead," Kim replied.

Carter made an ugly face.

"It couldn't be helped."

"No," he murmured, "I suppose it couldn't."

"What about this one, the one who was below with you?"

"I told you, she knows nothing. I'll handle her."

"Where will you send her?"

"San Francisco," he lied, "where she's from."

He searched the room until he found Tomiko's passport, her personal things, and a suitcase.

He put the money in the suitcase and piled clothes on top of it. When there was no more room, he shut it and walked down to the first floor.

"You'll get rid of the bodies?" he asked.

"Yes. We have already made the arrangements. When it is done, I will leave a man behind to fire the house."

Carter stopped at the front door. He turned to Kim Li and smiled. "You're very thorough."

"I once told you I was."

"Yeah, I remember."

"Nick . . ." She moved close until he could smell her perfume and the cordite tang that still hung in her clothes. "We won't be seeing each other again."

"No."

"It was better I did this myself."

"I know," he nodded. "That was why I let you do it."

He walked away from the sudden surprise on her face, moved down the steps, and got into the car. Tomiko was shivering in the passenger seat, her eyes darting everywhere at once.

"I am afraid," she whispered.

"Don't be," Carter said, swinging through the gates. "In fact, honey, if you're as smart as I think you are, you're never gonna have to be afraid for the rest of your life."

# EIGHTEEN

Carter stayed on the expressway right through Seoul and took the cutoff to Kimpo Airport. He parked and grabbed the bag.

"C'mon!"

He guided Tomiko into the terminal and up to the KAL counter.

"We called earlier. Tomiko Mochiko, your San Francisco flight?"

"Yes, sir. Passports, please."

Tomiko fidgeted as the passport was checked.

"You are a Japanese citizen. Will this be a round-trip ticket?"

"No," Carter answered. "She has relatives in San Francisco. She'll be staying awhile."

"Of course." The machine clicked as the ticket was printed. "Baggage?"

"Just one piece," Carter said. "She'll carry it on."

"Cash or charge?"

"Cash," Carter replied, smiling, "dollars."

"Fine. That will be fifteen hundred and seventy dollars."

Carter poked Tomiko in the ribs. "Pay the nice lady, honey."

Tomiko swallowed and laid out sixteen one-hundred-dollar bills on the counter.

"There, see how easy that was?" Carter said when it was over and they were walking toward the gate.

"I'm still scared."

"Don't be. When you get off in Tokyo, don't change planes. Just go out the terminal door and keep going. Lose yourself, Tomiko. Tear up the second half of that ticket, go hide someplace, and buy a business."

"So much money. . ."

"You earned it." They arrived at the gate. "This is it."

She turned sad eyes to his face. "I will never see you again, will I?"

"No, and you don't want to," Carter said gently. "It's best."

She looked at him for a long moment, then nodded. "Yes, I know."

"And a word to the wise. Forget all of this, understand? It never happened."

"Some of it happened."

She came up on her toes and fastened her lips to his. Her mouth was soft and pliant and faintly moist beneath his. After a moment, she thrust her tongue deep into his mouth and moved it vigorously.

As quick as the kiss started, it ended. Without a word, she turned and joined the crowd moving to the jetway.

Carter watched until he could no longer see her bobbing head, then turned and left the terminal.

He drove to the military intelligence headquarters in

downtown Seoul and presented his State Department credentials to the MP at the gate.

"Carter, State, to see Colonel Raymond Burgess."

"Yes, sir, your name is on the list. Building E to your right, sir."

Carter parked and did the same credentials number with a blond WAC lieutenant who all by herself could put uniforms in style for the next round of Paris shows.

"Right this way, Mr. Carter. The colonel has been expecting you."

The office was plush, carpeted, with shiny new intercom equipment and drapes at the window. Detailed maps covered the left wall, pictures of generals the right. The colonel's desk was some sleekly expensive wood, polished to a deep gloss. There were two wooden baskets on the desk, marked In and Out, both empty. The colonel's letter opener was a black-handled samurai sword done in miniature.

Bird Colonel Raymond Burgess was all iron jaw, muscles, and ribbons. He looked more John Wayne than John Wayne as he shook Carter's hand and motioned him to a chair. As Carter sat, he swung around behind his desk to sit in the padded swivel. He picked up the little sword and toyed with it. Carter noticed that a faint light gleamed at the front of one of the intercom boxes, and he'd bet that the colonel's lower desk drawer contained a going tape recorder.

"All right, Carter, I've had hot-line calls all morning from Washington. My ass was dragged out of bed at oh-four-hundred. God knows, I hope I'm going to be glad you're here at last."

"I can realize the problems, Colonel. I know this is all rather awkward."

"Awkward, shit! I've got over a hundred of my best

men on alert, some already at it, and I don't know what the hell is going on!"

"In time, Colonel," Carter replied. "First of all, have you got the house in Seoul and the one in Pusan under observation?"

"Hell, yes, around the clock. There are more taxi cabs, bread trucks, and telephone repairmen in those neighborhoods than there are residents!"

Carter sat back with a sigh and lit a cigarette. "Good, and they know what to do?"

"Believe me, Carter, everyone going in or out of those houses . . . they take a crap, we know it in five minutes. Now—"

Carter held up his hand. "Colonel, tonight there is going to be a meeting between some North Koreans and some South Koreans."

"Where?"

"That I don't know. But I would guess up near the DMZ."

"Impossible."

Carter sat back. "That's what I thought, a few days ago . . ."

Carter waited, silent and controlled, his motionless form blending perfectly with the night darkness of the hillside. The only sound to disturb the unnatural silence came from the labored breathing of the men around him. Suddenly, the moon slid from behind a cloud, its cold light etching the scene a thousand yards below them in stark relief.

The farmhouse and outbuildings seemed to blend into the far hillside, but with the nightglasses every detail could be seen clearly.

The Koreans under Colonel Burgess's command had done one hell of a job on motorcycles, produce trucks, and a half-dozen camouflage vehicles. They had tracked all three of the blue vans when they had left the safe house in Seoul. Two of the vans had been decoys. As soon as the right van had been identified, Carter and Burgess's tactical group had swung into operation.

By the time the van had pulled into the farm area and disappeared into the ramshackle barn, the team was in place. That had been two hours ago. In that time, the outpost sentries had been located. A sensor team had moved north from the farmhouse over a mile to the beginning of the DMZ. And four Toyota pickups with wooden manure vats in their beds had arrived and arranged themselves near the barn.

Now Carter, Burgess, and a young lieutenant lay tensely, waiting word from the sensor team to the north.

"Movement, sir," the lieutenant whispered suddenly.

Carter and Burgess both nodded. They adjusted their glasses and watched the pickup drivers form a line from the door of the barn to the trucks.

For twenty minutes, they watched oilskin packages handed from the door of the barn and loaded in the ordure-filled vats.

"What the hell . . . ?" Burgess hissed.

"I'd guess that every one of those packages is filled with counterfeit money, Colonel."

"Jesus."

"What better way to move it across the country? No one is going to stop those trucks and dip their hands in all that crap to see if they are carrying contraband."

There was the sound of movement behind them. All three heads turned to see a sergeant crawling toward them.

"Sir . . ."

"Yes, Sergeant?"

"Sensor team reports Mr. Carter's guess was correct. There is a tunnel running from under the barn north into the DMZ. They figure it's about seven high by four wide, and wood-beam supported."

"Well, I'll be damned," Burgess growled. "They built another one right under our noses."

"My hunch is it's only recently been finished, and its principal reason is more for those meetings and moving contraband," Carter said.

"It's your show, Carter," the colonel said.

"Rig it," Carter replied.

"Sergeant?"

"Yes, sir?"

"Pass the word to the team. Rig the tunnel with explosives. Sight detonation when I give the word."

"Yes, sir."

The sergeant slithered down the hill and Carter passed his glasses to the lieutenant.

"You know the drill, Colonel. You won't be needing me any more."

Burgess, from his years in the military, went over his orders.

"The van's occupants are allowed to go on their way. When they are definitely in the clear, the tunnel is to be blown. The trucks are to be followed to their destination and picked up there. Cleanup here takes place when the tunnel goes."

"Right," Carter said.

"Two questions . . ."

"Shoot," Carter said.

"One, what if the North Korean brass are still in the tunnel when we blow it?"

Carter smiled. "Fuck 'em."

"Good enough. Two, if the people in the van are the

honchos, how come we're letting them get away?"

The question gave Carter pause. He couldn't tell the colonel the whole truth, yet he figured he owed the man some explanation.

"Colonel, not long ago someone told me that when the head is severed, the body will mold. Here we have a delicate problem. We don't want the U.S. military involved in severing the head."

Carter left it at that, and moved down the hill. Burgess was no dummy. From the look on the man's face, Carter was pretty sure he got the picture.

"Sergeant?"

"Yes, sir?"

"Radio the air base at Kisai and tell them I'm on my way. Have the plane ready."

"Yes, sir."

Carter crawled into the Jeep and nodded to the driver. As they drove off, he stretched out in the narrow seat and forced his body to relax.

But he let his mind work, hard.

He was going over each step of the plan he had already formulated from the moment he would get off the plane in Hong Kong.

# NINETEEN

Six blocks away, Hong Kong harbor blazed with light and sound. A string of low-watt bulbs outlining the upper structure of an American cruiser had been turned on, and they rocked gently with the movement of the ship in the water.

In a tacky bar across the street, Wo Chong knocked back his fifth whiskey of the night. Carter watched him order another, and sighed.

After two days and two nights of watching the man's every move, he knew that his would be his last drink of the night.

Ten minutes later, he watched as the man stumbled from the bar, made his way two doors down the street, and went up to his apartment.

Carter lit a cigarette and killed another half hour in his darkened doorway. When the light in the third-floor window went out, he waited fifteen more minutes and crossed the street.

At the top of a rickety set of stairs, he moved directly to the door of Chong's apartment and listened. There was the sound of music turned low on a radio. Over the music he heard snoring.

Earlier that day, Carter had been at this same door to make a plastic impression of the locks. Now he had a key.

The vestibule and hall were dark. There was illumination from a low-watt bulb in the bedroom to the right.

Wo Chong lay like a beached whale on his back, naked save for a pair of boxer shorts. Carter placed the barrel of the Luger between Chong's eyes and gently squeezed the man's shoulder.

The eyes opened, registered on the gun, then stared beyond it at the ski mask over Carter's face. After a long stare, he moved his arms across his chest, hugging himself as though he wanted to ward off injury. He licked his lips and coughed slightly.

"Don't make a sound or I'll put your brains all over the pillow. Understand?"

A slight nod.

"Get up, slowly, and sit in that chair by the desk."

Wo Chong did as he was told as far as the chair. Then he got his nerve back and whirled.

Carter cracked the silencer across the side of his head and he folded. By the time he came around, his torso and his legs were secured to the chair with strips of sheet.

"What do you want?" he murmured groggily.

"I'll make it very clear. You are head of security at the Sea Breeze. As such, you were overseer of all those fancy electronic security systems up there."

Here Carter paused to pull a pad across the desk and set a stack of pencils in front of him.

"I want a schematic of the circuit system. I want the relay sequence from the main box, and I want the cutoff code for the bypasses. And don't give me any shit about not knowing them."

In answer, Wo Chong folded his arms over his chest.

"I don't have much time," Carter growled.

Silence.

"Okay, Chong, it's up to you."

Carter took a can of lighter fluid from his pocket. He started at the man's head and worked down over his body until the can was empty. Then he stepped back and flicked his lighter.

"You have three seconds. One . . ."

The man started scrawling on the pad.


Carter rolled over the edge of the roof and dropped silently to the balcony outside the third-floor dining room.

So far, everything had worked as smoothly as the mechanism of a Swiss watch.

From the main box outside the wall, he had jimmied the alarm circuit breakers so that he could get into the grounds undetected. At the secondary box in the basement, he had reset the pulsator codes to manual. A static pulsar on the main telephone box rendered communications in and out of the complex useless.

Then he had made his way to the first floor where the electronic office was. When he was sure all the night employees were in the big computer room, he manually shut and locked the doors from the outside.

When the three servants were bound and gagged, he made his way to the roof above the living quarters.

Now he waited on the balcony. They were at the table, picking at plates of food and talking earnestly.

Carter waited until the big Korean with the two steel claws for hands came into the room carrying a tray of desserts. Then he stepped through the door and shot the servant twice in the chest with the silenced Luger.

Pak San Roo was momentarily stunned. Kim Li dived

for a panel of buttons by the door. Carter let her punch the key-codes that would alert the gate guards.

"No good," Carter growled. "The circuits are bypassed. They'll get a steady beat down there. The house is secure except for the two steel doors coming up from the second floor. Close them!"

"Why are you doing this?" she said, her voice cool.

Carter moved to Pak and placed the snout of the Luger's silencer against his spine. "Go close the doors," he said, his eyes never leaving Kim's face. "Both circuits. Then come back."

"What if I don't know how to close the doors?" she said.

Carter sighed wearily. "Then I might as well shoot him now and get it over with. You know how to close the doors. Do it."

Pak's thin voice begged, "Please...Kim..." and something incoherent in Korean. She stood for another long moment before she went away.

Carter heard the sighs and clicks of the doors closing in sequence. He didn't relax his guard. When she returned he still held the pistol firm against Pak's spine.

"If anyone else is locked in here with us," he said, "or managed to get in, he'd better know now that Pak dies at the first sign of an attempt to rescue him."

"Nobody else is here. Nobody else can get in without being admitted," she said stonily. "Why are you doing this?"

"Because it's my job and I don't like to be suckered." He checked Pak quickly for a weapon. There was nothing to find. To Kim he said, "Take off your dress and toss it to me."

She hesitated, her eyes glittering icily, then complied. The dress was a silk *cheongsam* that he could ball in one

hand. Nothing was hidden in it; nothing potentially dangerous could have been hidden in the white panties that were
her other garment. He tossed the dress back to her.

"Sit over there where I can watch you both. Not too
close to him. Not too far away."

She obeyed again, silently. She didn't put on the dress,
which brought a slight smile to Carter's face. Her body was
as physically beautiful as it had always been, but now that
he knew the rot inside it, he felt nothing.

"This is foolish, Mr. Carter. You can't defy destiny."

"Can't I?" Calmly, Carter crossed to the bar and poured
three fingers of scotch into a glass. Then he slid onto a
stool where he could watch them both.

The initial shock had worn off. Pak's color was normal
again, his voice controlled. "It is inevitable that the two
Koreas will be reunited, Mr. Carter. It will never happen
from the South, only from the North, by force, when chaos
reigns in the South."

"And with all that counterfeit money, you bring on the
chaos, right?" Carter said, sipping his drink.

"You could be a part of it," Kim Li said, standing and
twisting her golden body to best show it off. "*We* could be
a part of it."

"Sit down!" Carter barked. "Part of it, eh? I should trust
you, the man who ordered his own son's death? And you,
the sister who was sent to kill him?"

Pak lit a cigarette and inhaled deeply. "How did you
find out?"

"The portrait of Kim Li. I went to the artist, Sing Hee
Youl. He sold me the sketches of both paintings, and gave
me names. The name of the father, Pak San Roo, the
daughter, Kim Li Roo, and the son, Tong Li Roo. He told
me you had the boy's painting destroyed."

Pak waved the cigarette in his hand. "He was no longer

my son. He was a disgrace, a homosexual, a thief to his own family."

"He was also smarter than hell, and ambitious," Carter growled. "When you eased him out, he got his hands on all your records and started moving in. He still hadn't accumulated all your power, but he was coming close. You wanted him dead, but you couldn't find him. It would have been useless to just kill Bonner. Tong Li would have found another Bonner somewhere. You needed someone from outside . . . me."

"And I must say," Pak replied with a slight smile, "you did your job well."

"Yeah, I sure as hell did."

"If you think it was so horrible, why did you give me the information?" Kim asked.

Carter finished his drink. "Because he had to go, and if you did it, I knew it made my theory about Dr. Kwon complete."

"And what theory was that?" Pak asked.

"What you told me that first night here. It was all bullshit. You never stopped being Dr. Kwon, Pak. You still had all the power, the contacts, the resources. All those safe houses we used in Seoul and Pusan. If your son had been as powerful as you said, Kim couldn't have operated as easily as she had. And you, Kim, it was so important that I see your brother's body, so that I could tell my government that Dr. Kwon was finally dead."

Carter wiped his forehead with a towel from the bar.

Pak was smiling, the wise old phoenix who would always rise from the ashes. He lit a fresh cigarette from the butt of the old one. "What do you want, Carter, in exchange for our lives?"

"I want Dr. Kwon, all of him. You must keep a master

file of the organization . . . names, places, blackmail material to keep certain people in line."

Pak stayed cool. He seemed to digest this, think about it.

Kim Li made a split-second mistake. Her eyes darted to a painting of the Pomosa Temple and its surrounding shrines that hung over Carter's shoulder on the wall behind the bar.

"In exchange for what you ask, I assume I could keep my wealth?"

"Father . . ."

"Be quiet," Pak barked. "This is a negotiation like any other. Well, Carter?"

Carter slid from the stool. He went around the bar and slid the painting aside. Behind it was a small Croland-Zeiss Swiss-made safe.

"I don't want or need your money, Pak. Open it."

"I'm afraid I would have to have more assurance than your word, Carter," the old man said evenly.

"Sorry," the Killmaster said, and shot him twice in the heart.

The heavy slugs knocked body and chair over together. The chair came to rest on top of the body, partially concealing it. From the stain of blood that quickly grew and spread around the chair, Pak's arm, hand, and limp fingers lay outstretched, pointing at Carter.

The woman made no sound. Both hands covered her face. She didn't cower in her chair, but sat erect. Carter knew from her breathing, the quick shallow rise and fall of her breasts, how she cringed inwardly at the imminence of her own death. But she made no gesture of appeal for mercy.

"Open the safe, Kim. If you don't do it, I will. It's a

three-tumbler Croland-Zeiss. It will take me about an hour, but I can get it open."

She moved like a robot to the safe. Her fingers on the dial were steady. Too steady.

"You don't have to die, Kim. Enough of you is already dead on the floor over there."

He heard the last tumbler click and she reached for the release handle.

"You're the father's daughter, but without him and what's in that safe, you can't re-create what he built."

The door swung open.

"Dr. Kwon is dead, Kim."

She had the automatic halfway around, the safety off, when Carter pumped three bullets from the Luger into her heart.

# DON'T MISS THE NEXT NEW
# NICK CARTER SPY THRILLER

## *MIDDLE EAST MASSACRE*

The Killmaster lay on his back in the bed of the small truck. Through the small rear window of the cab he could see both their heads. Ugly Mohab drove. Yushi Nuhr sat in the passenger seat.

They hadn't bothered to blindfold him after all. But then why should they? He wasn't coming back anyway, any more than he was going to Israel.

During the first half hour of the ride, the woman had glanced back to check on him several times. After she seemed assured that Carter had no intention of throwing himself off the rear of the truck, she kept her eyes forward.

It was a rough ride over sand, rocks, and, now and then, a little-used track. Carter welcomed it. The bouncing around allowed him to get his back closer to the side of the truck bed. Once there, he could steady himself and get some leverage.

Once Hugo's sharp point had pierced his shirt, Carter scrunched his arms up to the small of his back. On the first two tries he missed and sliced the heels of his hands.

The third time he made it and began to saw on the ropes. The stiletto was razor-sharp, so it wasn't long before he felt his wrists part.

Gingerly, he grasped the blade between thumb and forefinger. Despite the chill of the desert night, his back was sweat-slick. The knife slid easily from under the gauze.

He went to work on the rope that bound his ankles. It was tricky. He didn't want to cut all the way through the rope, just enough strands so that when he came off the truck bed he could pop them by yanking his legs apart.

During all of this he had kept track of their position by the stars. The route Mohab had taken was almost due west. Once he had cut north for about three miles, only to head directly west again.

Why not? Carter thought. They didn't fear him pinpointing the missile site. He wasn't coming back.

When there was only one strand holding his ankles together, he brought the stiletto back up to the small of his back.

He turned his eyes back toward the front. The headlights lit a bumpy, rutted road that seemed to lead toward a black abyss. The longer they drove, the more bumpy, the more primitive it became.

Carter winced as the truck scraped over heavy rocks that kicked up and thumped and banged along the undercarriage. Mohab was heading into hilly country where it appeared no vehicle had ever been before.

As the truck creaked and groaned over one violent bump after another, it threw Carter high enough off the truck bed so he could see Mohab dodging boulders along the dusty trail.

The truck headed down a steep hill toward a black hole of a valley. The thumping from the rocks stopped, to be

replaced with a staccato *flap flap flap* as they drove into a
sand wadi off the rocky trail.

Mohab pulled on the emergency brake and killed the
engine. They both got out of the cab and moved around the
truck. Carter heard the woman cock the AK-47 she carried.

At the rear of the truck, Yushi Nuhr stood off a couple
of feet, the assault rifle across her chest. Mohab moved
toward Carter.

"Are we near the river?" Carter asked, holding his
ankles tightly together.

"As close as you're going to get," the woman barked.
"Put him on the ground!"

The big Arab leaned his rifle against the side of the
truck, put the cigarette he was smoking in his lips, and
reached for Carter.

He grabbed the Killmaster by the ankles and yanked
him off the truck bed like a side of beef.

Carter howled as his backside scraped painfully over the
rough boards. He fell heavily to the sand.

Mohab backed off, leisurely smoking his cigarette. The
woman moved in. Carter got to his knees.

"You're going to kill me, aren't you," he said.

The woman smiled. The evil in her face was almost
beautiful in it simplicity. "Like a dog."

She was bringing the gun around, when Carter sprang.
The stiletto came up like an uppercut. It entered her body
just beneath her left breast. Carter felt her blood gush over
his hand and forearm.

Her eyes widened and she gasped as the pain followed
the shock. By instinct, she slammed the rifle down across
Carter's arm.

He hadn't expected it. At the same time, she rolled
away from him, pulling the blood-slick hilt of the stiletto
from his grasp.

Mohab's reflexes were lightning fast. A howl erupted from his throat as he left his feet in a dive for his own rifle leaning against the truck.

Carter swung in a complete circle. The toe of his boot caught the big man in the middle of his face. Mohab howled in pain and rolled when he hit the sand.

Carter contemplated going for the rifle himself, but Mohab was already back on his feet, charging. The Kill-master set himself to sidestep the bulllike charge and put a knee into the other man's groin.

He didn't expect what happened.

Mohab paused in mid-charge and moved into a fighter's stance, a wolfish grin twisting his ugly lips.

"This is better. I will beat you to death with my hands."

Carter was surprised, too surprised. Before he knew it, his head was rocked back with a couple of stinging punches that landed over his right eye.

Blood immediately filled his eyes. He shook his head to clear it.

He couldn't believe the incongruity of it as Mohab moved around him, cutting him off from both rifles. The man actually meant what he said: he was going to kill Carter with his bare hands.

All Carter could do was fight fire with fire and try to maneuver himself back toward one of the rifles. This would be easier said than done. Mohab had fifty pounds and five inches of reach on him. And the man glided in the soft sand like a snake.

Carter threw himself forward. Mohab went low, bobbed to his left, and let Carter's clubbing right hand go past. The Arab leaned into his own right and dug it into Carter's body just under the ribs. Carter turned and the hook caught him with the weight of Mohab's big body behind it.

Carter shook his head. Blood seeped down from a split

eyebrow. The left hand rapped him twice, three more times before he could pull his head behind a shoulder.

The Arab was good.

"Come!" the big man taunted, a leering grin curving his thick lips. "Do not back up! Fight!"

Pivoting, Carter aimed a kick at his kneecap, a savage sweep of the foot that would have crippled him if it had landed. Mohab stuck the left into Carter's mouth, shifted it to the sore right eye, and hooked off the jab as he skipped away. Carter plodded after, pulling air into his lungs, knowing already the first heaviness in his legs, needing to close with Mohab to hold him and work him over before he could pull away. Mohab had to be slowed down.

The left again, educated, a slashing weapon that was cutting Carter's face to pieces.

Carter lunged, tried to go into a shell as he came in, but Mohab stabbed and coasted back, stabbed and stopped momentarily to bang both hands to Carter's body, to switch the jolting hook to Carter's jaw. Then he was gone again.

Carter focused on the man's smirking face, on the untouched face with the coldly mocking eyes. Head down, he rammed in and almost caught Mohab solidly. His head glanced off the Arab's ribs, but when he tried to wrap an arm around his belly, something exploded against the back of his neck.

He fell, and a heavy boot ground his face into the sand. He sensed the other foot going back. Mohab was going to kick his skull in.

Carter hooked a desperate hand around an ankle and snapped it down and away. Mohab fought for balance, hissing like a cornered rattlesnake. He went down, but not hard, still good with his weight, still quick. He was rolling over when Carter got him in the back with a knee.

The big man yelped in shock, clawed at the truck to pull

himself out from under the sudden pain. Carter hit him twice, then again, both hands chopping behind the head, both hands driving Mohab into the sand.

But the man was tough. He was hard and rugged, and proved it by arching violently to hands and knees, by throwing Carter off his back. He scuttled away as Carter tried to grab him again, and used the truck to climb up. When he turned, Carter saw where the rough metal had scraped his face raw on one side, saw the new angle of Mohab's nose, the leaking blood.

He came off the back of the truck, using it as a fulcrum. He butted Carter in the face, but the Killmaster was past feeling blows. He rocked with it and chopped Mohab along the neck, then got his knee into the man's crotch. Mohab stopped. He lowered his head to Carter's pumping chest and hung on, wrapping his thick arms around Carter so he could stay on his feet.

Gulping a lungful of air, Carter pulled his arms free and got the right one around the Arab's neck in a headlock, anchoring the grip with his other hand. Mohab was tough. He'd taken the pain and the hammering and hadn't begged for mercy; he hadn't cried uncle.

But Carter saw that it wouldn't take much now to finish him.

He took a faltering run at the truck, with Mohab's head sticking out of his grip. Carter wobbled at the smash, used his hip to keep Mohab up, and backed away for another swaying try at the truck bed.

The second smash accomplished its purpose. Under Carter's left arm Mohab's head cracked sickeningly against the rear of the truck. When the Killmaster let him drop limply to the sand, Mohab's eyes were rolling and the top of his skull was spongy.

Carter leaned against the truck, gasping for air. His left

eye was blinded by blood now, and there was a mist in front of the right one. There wasn't a bone or muscle in his body that didn't scream with pain, and his legs felt as though they were hollow and filled with water.

He had to concentrate to keep from blacking out. It was unbelievable, but Mohab was still moving. Laboriously, the man crawled to one knee. Then he defied gravity and got to his feet.

*Impossible*, Carter thought, *the man is dead!*

To make it all worse, he heard a sound to his left. He turned and saw Yushi Nuhr. Somehow she was still alive, the stiletto protruding from beneath her breast.

She had crawled to her rifle and was trying to bring it into a position to fire.

"Give it up!" Carter gasped. "You're dead, or you should be!"

She was superhuman. It was as if she were a zombie, the walking dead. Her face was bloodless, the eyes already milky white. Yet she managed to lift the rifle.

At the same time, Mohab aped her. Like a robot he headed for Carter, his big paws in front of him, the fingers curling in anticipation of the Killmaster's throat.

It took Carter's last ounce of strength. He stumbled to the woman and grabbed the gun.

Useless.

Her grip on the rifle was with all the strength of death. The muzzle continued to roll in his direction. Behind him, he could hear Mohab's plodding steps toward him in the sand.

"Jesus," Carter croaked.

He lunged at the woman. He took her by her slender bird's throat with one hand, his thumb pushed in behind the point of her jawbone to paralyze her, his fingers cutting her wind. She could only pull without strength at his wrist, trying to take some of the pressure off the nerve center. It was instinctive but ineffectual. Only a counterattack against another nerve center, the testicles most vulnerable of all, could have broken his hold, and he held her in a way to defend himself against that. When she was helpless, he spun her into the deadly curve of his arms.

Laboriously, he lifted his knee into her back and bent her until he heard the neck snap.

Just before he pushed the woman's lifeless body into Mohab, he withdrew the stiletto from her breast.

The big Arab had to be sightless, but he shoved her off by instinct and kept staggering toward Carter. He grunted as he moved, saliva and blood drooling from the corners of his mouth.

But still he came.

Carter staggered himself. He moved his feet wide apart, the right foot a few inches behind the left for balance.

When Mohab embraced him, Carter buried the stiletto in his groin. With his last effort, he yanked upward, twisting the blade at the same time, disemboweling the big Arab.

There was no scream of agony, no wrenching of the body.

The man was already dead. He slid down Carter's front, leaving a bloody trail in his wake.

The Killmaster took two faltering steps and fell across both their bodies.

—From MIDDLE EAST MASSACRE
A New Nick Carter Spy Thriller
From Jove in May 1989

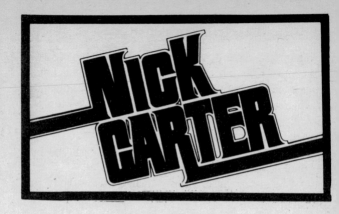